# Advance Praise for *Instant Karma:*

"Mark Swartz has written a remarkable book. *Instant Karma* is a quick, bright thing that is sort of hilarious, always amusing, somewhat edgy, thoroughly wry, genuinely touching, and very complicated. It's the History Channel of marvelous quotes from charming, smart people, and with it Swartz integrates fact and fiction effortlessly, so that both are enlarged, revised, extended.

*Instant Karma* is insta-good, a tour de force, an engaging, farcical, joyful reprise of a thousand great ideas tumbling around in one humble brain, in one ordinary body. It has a great, remarkable, explosive ending that explodes right into your heart. Buy it and keep it with you at all times."

> —Frederick Barthelme, author of *Painted Desert* and
> co-author of *Double Down*

"An obsessive read about an obsessive reader, Mark Swartz's *Instant Karma* is a book with the sort of power that makes you remember the sort of power books have."

> —Daniel Handler, author of *Watch Your Mouth* and
> *The Basic Eight*

"*Instant Karma* is irresistible from beginning to end. To make this original treatment of a complex and indeed zany subject so consistently entertaining is proof of a new and prodigious talent."

> —Harry Mathews, author of *Cigarettes* and *Tlooth*

"Funny, erudite, tender, and sad, *Instant Karma* traces the mental disintegration of a young man's journey from solitary bibliophile to Dada-library terrorist. But the book is also a meditation on our fragmented culture — that mysterious hodge-podge of conflicting images and myriad bits of text that threaten to destroy all possible meaning. In Mark Swartz's hapless anti-hero, David Felsenstein, the distance between incendiary idea and literal explosion becom                          gly real."
                                                               says and

D1292965

"What a pleasure it is to read a book that is so wholly itself — contained and furious, timely and profound, and deeply, rigorously smart. I underlined passage after passage, as Swartz synthesizes the voices of countless other authors with his own, making a book built of books, creating both castles and rubble in the reader's mind. A striking debut."

> —Aimee Bender, author of *The Girl in the Flammable Skirt* and *An Invisible Sign of My Own*

"*Instant Karma* reminds me of a number of my favorite books — Gogol's scary-funny *Diary of a Madman* comes to mind. But it's a special kind of madness, book madness, the terror and pleasure of reading that is conjured up, making one think of the novels of David Markson, the inspired frenzy of John Leonard's critical prose, and of course the great novel in footnotes *Pale Fire*. But *Instant Karma* is *sui generis:* Mark Swartz offers us an exploded library of crazy wisdom in brilliant fragments."

> —Ron Rosenbaum, author, *Explaining Hitler* and *The Secret Parts of Fortune*

"This novella proves that too much reading can cause a shy boy to use explosives. The attenuated Young Werther here, direct heir to all the neurasthenic adolescents in literature, updates himself with late-20th-century books, but stays in character. Nice satire, useful common reader."

> —Andrei Codrescu, NPR commentator and author of *Ay Cuba! A Socio-Erotic Journey* and *Casanova in Bohemia*

"As a reference librarian I have sometimes wondered what goes on in the hearts and minds of the many people who use the library all day, every day. Swartz provides just such a glimpse into one fictional psyche. *Instant Karma*'s troubled protagonist's diary entries, obsessively footnoted from idiosyncratically disparate library texts, lead toward a potentially explosive end."

> —Jim Van Buskirk, Reference Librarian, San Francisco Public Library

# INSTANT KARMA

## BY MARK SWARTZ

CITY LIGHTS
SAN FRANCISCO

Cover image: Detail of "Attempt to Raise Hell" by Dennis
Oppenheim *(1974; cast-iron bell, wood and cloth seated figure,
timer)* has been reproduced with permission of the artist.
Private collection, Amarillo, Texas. Photo courtesy of Ace
Gallery, NY.

Cover design by Rex Ray
Book design by Elaine Katzenberger
Typography by Harvest Graphics

The cover of the *Chicago Reader* has been reproduced with the
permission of the *Chicago Reader* (© Chicago Reader, Inc., 1994)

Acknowledgments:

Excerpts of this work have previously appeared in *Chelsea* and
the *Brooklyn Rail*. The author would like to thank Laurel,
Michael, Robert, and Matthew Swartz, Jim Poniewozik, Michael
Cohen, Scott Cohen, Rob Preskill, Elaine Katzenberger, Stacey
Lewis, and, above all, Jennie Guilfoyle.

Library of Congress Cataloging-in-Publication Data

Swartz, Mark
    Instant karma / by Mark Swartz.
        p.    cm.
    Includes bibliographical references.
    ISBN 0-87286-408-1 (pbk.)
Libraries and readers—Fiction.    2.  Public libraries—Fiction.
3.  Chicago    (Ill.)—Fiction.    4.  Mentally ill—Fiction.
I. Title.
PS3619.W37 I57 2002
813'.6—dc21                                    2002073841

**Visit our web site: www.citylights.com**

CITY LIGHTS BOOKS are edited by Lawrence Ferlinghetti and
Nancy J. Peters and published at the City Lights Bookstore,
261 Columbus Avenue, San Francisco, CA 94133

To librarians everywhere

### Saturday 5 November 1994

Guy Fawkes Day, a good starting point for the journal of an anarchist. "A desperate disease requires a dangerous remedy," Fawkes said.[1]

Robert Cecil, the first Earl of Salisbury, who executed Fawkes and seven others January 30–31, 1606, for conspiring to blow up Parliament, said, "The greater the offences are, the more hydden they lie."[2] But if an offense, public, private, historic, contemporary, is so great then it can withstand any amount of attention. If a hidden one can stay hidden, then it couldn't be that great. A man who has cancer in his body undiagnosed throughout his life until a truck runs him over, wasn't a cancer victim.

### Sunday 6 November

Bluefin tuna "carry particles of magnetite in their brains that allow them to navigate using the earth's magnetic field."[3] I am sure that other creatures, such as elephants, have evolved analogous navigational tools, magnetic or otherwise. Such apparatus varies widely in human subjects. My own deficiency in this regard leaves me as disabled as a deaf-mute or a hemophiliac—perhaps more so, since it's ignored by the same medical establishment that funds research into chronic fatigue syndrome and sudden infant death syndrome. I have no faith in syndromes, not excluding the big one.

---

[1] Dictionary of National Biography.

[2] Quoted in Mark Nicholls, *Investigating Gunpowder Plot* (Manchester: Manchester University Press, 1991), p. ix.

[3] John Seabrook, "Death of a Giant," *Harper's* (June 1994): p. 53.

My biochemical disorientation was a family joke. My parents would tell friends that if I didn't come back from a restaurant bathroom after a reasonable amount of time, they would know they could find me hovering between the kitchen and the broom closet. Entering a building through one door and exiting through another, I've never known which way to turn to get where I was going; and since I never think of myself as getting lost until it's too late to recall where exactly I went wrong, directional instinct betrays me even further, and every landmark easily reverses itself. Once I set out in one direction, no matter how far along I get, even if everything looks right, I feel unsure of my decision.

The sense of being lost quickly mutates into a self-hatred that has no parallel in any other phase of my existence. The names I call myself, the abuse I dish—if I weren't so upset, I'd laugh at myself grunting, "Hurray for the God-damned idiot! Hray!"[4] My disorientation increases with complexity of architecture, which is why M. C. Escher is a redundancy for me. Buildings with exits and entrances on different floors stymie me, as do elevators that open in front and back. Urban planners spend seven years in graduate school studying how others have ignored my condition in the past and devising new ways to perplex me in the future. They meet in city hall to dream up highway ramps aiming in contradictory loops, one-ways, and divided highways, and diagonal streets—

---

[4] Stephen Dedalus, in Joyce's *Ulysses*, ridicules himself with these words when he recalls the days of "reading two pages apiece of seven books every night" (New York: Random House, 1934), p. 41.

especially diagonal streets, which require a grasp of eight compass directions at once.

If not for the existence of the Israeli army, made up of Jews who presumably have the same genetic history as I do but zip across unmarked skies and deserts without having to think about it, I would be certain that the condition is racial.[5]

## Monday 7 November

Eve Jablom: a thing of beauty and a joy for none.

## Tuesday 8 November

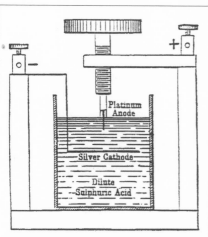

Fig. 2. Wide acceptance and usage of Fessenden's improved "liquid barretter" made it possible for many to hear his first radiotelephony broadcasts. (Figs. 1 and 2 from reference 5.)

Election Day. Do anarchists vote? They vote for everybody. And they stand outside polling places wearing Brooks Brothers suits and paper bags with holes cut out for the eyes, distributing leaflets with handwritten copies of poems and quotations by Gertrude Stein, Emma Goldman, and Hugo Ball. Anarchists sing patriotic songs off-key and pay compliments to ladies with hats and children

---

[5] Jews "aren't made for geographies but for histories" (Grace Paley, *Collected Stories* [New York: Farrar, Straus, Giroux, 1994]).

with glandular abnormalities. They spew meaningless statistics and warn voters not to eat the donuts that the polling officials are offering. Upon hearing election results on the radio, anarchists laugh themselves hoarse.

## Wednesday 9 November

In *Fahrenheit 451,* Ray Bradbury describes the members of the resistance as "bums on the outside, libraries inside."[6] In this city we have the reverse.

Eve ensures smooth operation of the library, and the library morally anchors the city. There, in the dialogue between texts, among the disputes fueled by dead ideas, the pictures in magazines, the closely argued papers in scholarly journals, mass accumulates, condenses, derives from itself the force of gravity that keeps the city from flying apart. Only to the extent that the police serve and protect the library do they separate society from anarchy. Most people never go to the library, but most people never go to the moon either, and the moon makes the waves in the ocean.

## Thursday 10 November

Eve gave me a look of knowing apprehension this evening when I checked out *Stephen Hero,* as if something she had been wondering earlier now made sense.[7] With a couple of keystrokes she could print out a list of every book I've ever checked out. I should consider this access as yet another invasion of privacy by government in the

---

[6] New York: Ballantine, 1953, p. 136.

[7] James Joyce, *Stephen Hero*: "There is an art, Mr. Dedalus, in lighting a fire" (New York: New Directions, 1944), p. 28.

Information Age, but instead I hope that what she'd see would impress her. A true Man of Letters! she'd think. A reader with a taste for the neglected classics of the past as well as the more obscure works of the great writers. Charlotte Brontë's *Villette* instead of her *Jane Eyre*. Kafka's diaries instead of his novels. Not *Hamlet*, *Titus Andronicus*.[8]

If she checks, she'll notice that Felsenstein, David E., never kept a book out past its due date. That ought to earn me a commendation in the library's quarterly newsletter.

### Friday 11 November

Today I accidentally walked out of the library without checking out Havelock Ellis's *Dance of Life*[9] and didn't even set off the alarm as I passed through the electronic gate. I wonder if this feat has something to do with the anti-magnet in my brain. Fine, if it happens in a library, but what about airports? Do the metal detectors ever blink? If I were a terrorist by occupation and was flying for pleasure only, and if I forgot to leave my grenade behind, and if airport security missed it, I would feel obligated to hijack the plane.

Though architecturally dissimilar, libraries and airports promote similar worldviews. Sections are assigned alphanumeric codes, and passage down every corridor tests the skill and memory of the visitor, while workers push glum carts without having to look up to see where they are. Libraries are airports for people who aren't going anywhere and who are picky about what they read.

[8] "Come and take choice of all my library, / And so beguile thy sorrow" (IV.i.34-35).

[9] "The great writer . . . knows how to quote" (Boston: Houghton Mifflin, 1923), p. 152.

### Sunday 13 November

In the eleven Salvation Army doctrines,[10] there's no mention of couches sprayed with cat piss, bleach-stained velour shirts, Betamaxes, six-slice toasters, or tarnished heart-shaped cookie cutters. Purple suspenders and broken chair seats. What a revolting place.

No. 5: "We believe that our parents were created in a state of innocency [sic] but by their disobedience they lost their purity and happiness and that in consequence of their fall all men have become sinners totally depraved and as such are justly exposed to the wrath of God." No. 10: "We believe that it is the privilege of all believers to be 'wholly sanctified' and that 'their whole spirit and soul and body' may 'be preserved unto the coming of the Lord Jesus Christ.'"

And my favorite, No. 11: "We believe in the immortality of the soul, in the resurrection of the body, in the general judgment at the end of the world, in the eternal happiness of the righteous, and in the endless punishment of the wicked." Respectively: yes, no, no, no, no.

### Monday 14 November

D. Edgar Felsenstein, the first Salvation Army bell ringer with anarchist leanings. I told Mr. Leon, a man whose corduroys are worn smooth on the tops of his thighs but who denies himself the bounty offered by the thrift shop, that I was good at handling change. He said he sees a little bit of himself in me. I told him the holiday season excited me, and

---

[10] Herbert A. Wisbey, Jr., *Soldiers without Swords* (New York: MacMillan, 1955), pp. 219-20.

he laughed in a way that made me think I had accidentally made a bawdy remark. Get a lot of action around Christmas, Mr. Leon? Tis the season if you know what I mean. You don't have to spell out for me the reason your pants are worn out.

For me, bell ringing doesn't serve any amorous function. I'd die if Eve saw me, but why would Eve ever stroll down Michigan Avenue? She's a State Street girl. No, bell ringing has nothing to do with her. It's the opportunity to keep time as the momentum picks up, as the shoppers grow frenzied and their children suffocate under layers of Thinsulate. There must be more to buy, there must be more to buy. The crowds thicken. The homeless send out for reinforcements. It gets noisy. Cars make sudden turns into walls of pedestrians. At first, people smile at one another, but by mid-December they're shoving, stealing, tipping over stacks of argyle sweaters. And the weather outside is frightful. And there's still room on my charge card, so get the hell out of my way. Capitalism shades into Anarchy.

Drop your coins in my can, sir, and your change will go to the building of pipe bombs for the federal court house and a huge electromagnet to sabotage the phone lines and disrupt cable television transmissions. Hear the chaotic clanging of my bell and dodge my spit and invectives, you bitches and sons of bitches. Why should I thank you, ma'am, when our intercourse is repugnant to me and gratifying for you? Why should I smile? Why should I even let you see my face? The least I can do for you is to make the recipient of your charity unknown to you.[11]

---

[11] Maimonides, in his Laws of Gifts for the Poor, 10:7 in *Mishneh Torah,* values anonymity in giving *tzedakah.*

The "Hustle" *War Cry* cover captured the Army's desire to be both up-to-date and effective. AWC, Oct. 10, 1896, 1, SAA

There are several good reasons for wearing a paper bag over my head while I swing that bell like an ax. The Salvation Army people will have to show me where it says I can't wear a bag.

### Tuesday 15 November

Collected $44.71 today. My breathing dampened the inside of the bag. My right shoulder aches, and my right ear is ringing, ringing.

### Wednesday 16 November

Mr. Leon says that customers have been asking questions about me. The paper bag scares them. In the back of the store he sat me down and asked if I knew what I looked like to people with a bag on my head. He stood over me to peer down into my face and grimace.

"Do you?"

"No, sir."

"Is it the fumes from the traffic? Are you an asthmatic, Dave? There was an asthmatic last year who wore a surgical mask."

"No, sir, I like the city air. Especially when a bus rumbles past. Buses use ethanol and it burns clean."

"Are you embarrassed to ring the bell? A lot of brave and honorable men have rung that bell. Soldiers without swords. Afraid your girlfriend's going to see you in the red smock?"

"No. She. Never mind. I'm not embarrassed. I didn't think it would be a big deal. It's not in the 11 Salvation Army Doctrines."

A pause. He never read them, never even heard of them. "I'm saying it doesn't look good. Do you know what it looks like?"

"No, sir."

How can I know what it looks like? All I can tell is what people look like to me when I see them through the eye-holes in the bag. They look farther away, and the colors are brighter and flattened-out like cartoons. I suppose optics have something to do with it. How do I look to people, Mr. Leon? I suppose I look like a combination town crier, nightwatchman, and executioner.

### Thursday 17 November

I spent the entire evening reading the video catalog that arrived in today's mail. There are so many movies; I'm sure we've reached the point where a person could be brought up in a screening room, all the hours of his entire life watching nothing but movies, skipping meals, an education, a career, sitting in the dark watching nothing but movies, eight per day—or twelve per day if it went on during sleep, and why shouldn't it? That person would grow accustomed to the codes and patterns that belong to the history of film and eventually believe that he controlled them, and in his confusion he would come to see himself as the vengeful and petty God of the Old Testament. Or at least as a studio boss who sees himself as God.[12] I circled more than forty in the catalog, and this in

---

[12] In *An Empire of Their Own,* Neal Gabler writes, "The Hollywood Jews created a powerful cluster of images and ideas—so powerful that, in a sense, they colonized the American imagination" (London: WH Allen, 1988, pp. 6-7).

itself is a pleasurable activity—making calligraphic Os, incomplete; the two ends must miss each other. I ordered only two, hoping it would be okay to send cash. The first is *1941* (1979) Spielberg's other World War II farce, featuring John Belushi at his coked-up best, a film with a lot of shouting and explosions in it.

The second is *The Lord's Prayer*, the only film made by Salim Sultan, an Indian-born poet who served a life sentence for burning down a Catholic church in London in 1920. The catalog says that there was only one print of the film made, and that was thought to be destroyed by psychiatrist/memoirist/drummer Richard Huelsenbeck during a poetry reading at the Cabaret Voltaire in 1916, but it resurfaced in Texas in the 1970s and was kept by an oil magnate who screened it every year at the company Christmas party so religious types would know they weren't welcome. The catalog says that the opening sequence of D. A. Pennebaker's 1965 documentary on Bob Dylan, *Don't Look Back*, showing the frail singer displaying cue cards with the approximate lyrics to his "Subterranean Homesick Blues," pays homage to *The Lord's Prayer*, though how Dylan or Pennebaker could have possibly viewed the film during its period of unavailability is unclear.

### Friday 18 November

Eve has been overworked and inhospitable, just like the Mary that George Bailey never married. Muscles clench in her temples when she tries to smile. She seems close to the edge. How would a librarian act during a nervous breakdown? Would she remember to remain quiet? Don't be afraid, Eve, it's the easiest thing in the world. Think of it as accepting a dare. I dare you to laugh out loud for no reason at all. Now, I dare you to topple that stack of books. I double dare you to lose your mind.

### Saturday 19 November

Product engineers have developed electronic ringers to the point where they are no longer so distinguishable from real bells. The phone in the apartment upstairs has been ringing all evening long. I am sure that I hear movement up there as well. I don't think that Mrs. Bryars is out at all. She just isn't answering the phone. Whoever is calling, probably Mr. Bryars, who moved out seven years ago, knows that she is home, and he is sitting in a room somewhere, the receiver to his ear, listening to the ringing and picturing her sitting by the phone listening to the ringing. He imagines that listening to the same sound (not quite but almost) brings them together in a way that words failed to. There is a ring and then silence, a ring and then silence. A conversation of two words. The ring is "please" and the silence is "no." Puh-lease. No. Puh-lease. No. Puh-lease. Maybe he thinks he's getting somewhere with her. That eventually his pleas will be heard and she'll pick up the phone and say, "Okay."

### Sunday 20 November

I left grad school because I was sick of adhering to the syllabi my professors distributed at the beginning of a quarter. I'd look over the list of titles and page ranges, resenting the fact that my reading for the next ten weeks was scheduled in advance by someone I hardly knew. Reading, for me, is a very personal decision comprised of whims, predispositions, and circumstances that I myself can't always pin down, and I didn't have any more confidence that Hegel, Marx, and Nietzsche would suit me two months in the future than that a bagel, lox, and cream cheese would hit the spot the following Sunday morning. Sometimes the library's 1.6 million books paralyze me; I don't know where to start and would welcome the guidance of a more experienced scholar. Other times I can be very single-minded. For example, I know that tomorrow when the library doors open I will race in and head right for Capote's *In Cold Blood*, the criminal mind and its expression in literary form being a topic that concerns me lately.

### Monday 21 November

Today I neared the counter to inform Eve that the men's room on the second floor was out of paper towels, but then I noticed her fingers. She was folding overdue notices, and I noticed how shiny her fingers were. Not greasy, but almost plastic-coated, laminated, like everything else in that place. I watched her as she pushed the overdue notices to one side and put her hands together— not in prayer, but so that the fingertips of one hand were just touching the fingertips of the other hand. I knew that if she concentrated, she could feel her blood pulsating, and I was struck dumb by the idea of its rhythm.

"Yes?" she said, not smiling, but not impatiently.

"I'm sorry."

"You look lost."

"No I don't," I said. I tried to laugh but could not. I don't know why I contradicted her. I wasn't in a position to know how I looked. I took her honest solicitation as a rebuke and panicked. Lost? I should have said. Lost like the more than 150,000 books that were lost in the transition from the library on Randolph? At least I didn't say that.

She picked up on my half-smile and saved the day: "That's good, because we wouldn't want to lose you."

### Tuesday 22 November

If I read enough books I will come across justification for everything that occurs to me. Every student leaning over his books reads with one eye dutifully scanning for material related to the immediate task and one eye searching for assurance of his deepest convictions. The book that contains the most wisdom is the one that makes the most sense. The Talmud, that great how-to manual of ancient Babylon, instructs us to eat fish heads. "May it be your will, HaShem, our God and the God of our forefathers, that we be as the head and not the tail."[13] I'll tell the fishmonger they're for my cat. Now what's a good name for a cat?

Yah-weh
Marzipan
Karma
Ubu
Eve
Malloy
Tanya

---

[13] Horayot 12a; Kerisus 6a. *Art Scroll Siddur* (Brooklyn: Mesorah Publishing, 1984), p. 769.

## Wednesday 23 November

This is the time of year when Americans are supposed to begin suffering the holidays. A blue Thanksgiving, a black Christmas, and a suicidal New Year's Eve live from Times Square with Dick Clark. I am an American, and that means that I am entitled to whatever armory I can stock and that I can't take responsibility for my actions. Am I blue? Ain't this *Guns & Ammo* telling you?

This endeavor will take the form of art. I have an urge, not just to write incendiary prose or create a blazing spectacle, but to ignite, detonate, explode. In *The Anarchist Cookbook,* William Powell tells of "a friend who worked with demolitions in the Middle East, and he has told me on several occasions that an explosion for him was an experience very similar to a sexual orgasm."[14] I've got a big woody for some hot flames, and I want to sublimate it into art. Lacking the necessary grudge to be a serial bomber, I would like to take all the time in the world preparing for the one-time-only event; but in the thriller tradition, there is a race afoot, so I can't wait too long. I am playing the Dennis Hopper role, the mad bomber with the oddly cogent sense of justice, but I am also Clint Eastwood. On the force they regard me as a straight shooter, but deep down I feel a kinship with the bomber and envy his charisma. My only weapon a pen. Will I write my way to reason? Can I come up with the precise combination of words and sentences to avert disaster before time runs out?

---

[14] Powell, *The Anarchist Cookbook* (Secaucus: Barricade Books, 1989), p. 112.

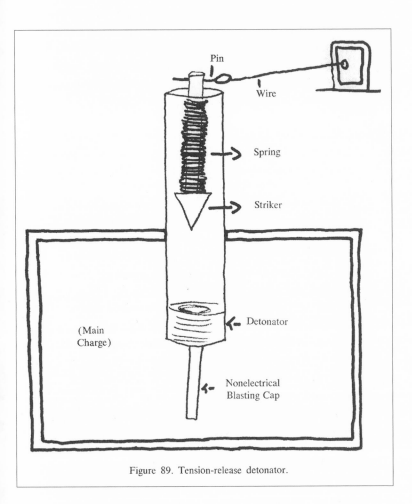

Figure 89. Tension-release detonator.

The late twentieth century is crowded with such media-hungry terrorists as myself. I can't speak for any of the others—we haven't yet held conventions—but I am tired of *terrorism* being treated as a political strategy, when at the very least it is a complete political ideology, on a par with Libertarianism or Marxism. I would go further and say that it might also be considered a religion,[15] whose gods are technology, power, and publicity. Like a religion, it requires discipline and self-sacrifice. Like a religion, simple statements of fact lurk behind bewildering arcana. Like a religion, everything depends on faith.

For my personal use, I think that *terrorism* will best be defined as an artistic movement,[16] a trend in creativity with progenitors, leaders, and marginal figures who make crucial contributions. Terrorism grew out of abstract expressionism and dadaism. Like the Helmites in Solomon Simon's tale, who saw the reflection of the moon in a tub of red borscht and convinced themselves they had captured the moon, the abstract expressionists made a few violent brushstrokes and thought they had captured the essence of destruction. They gestured bigger and more violently, swiping and stabbing at the canvas, dripping industrial paint like blood. Unfortunately, when blood dries, its loses its brilliance.

---

[15] "It was necessary that terrorism become a mystic cult" (André Malraux, *Man's Fate* [New York: Vintage], 1961, p. 182). And Robin Morgan says that "religion is about terror" (in her *Demon Lover*, New York: Norton, 1989, p. 88). Vice versa.

[16] Jillian Becker says, "The aestheticization of politics . . . is still alive and working in terrorists" (*Terrorism* 4 [1980]: p. 318).

If abstract expressionism is Oroboros, the mythical snake eternally consuming its own tail, then dadaism is an actual fish—stinking, slippery, and stiff enough that the tail won't meet the savory head. The dadaists started strong, with Alfred Jarry back in the last *fin de siècle,* wearing a mask and shooting real bullets at Parisian streetlamps. Jarry cleared the way for the likes of Hugo Ball. Creating art that is anti-art is nice; it will get you into the museums, but the real trick is creating art that is anti-life. Ball wrote, "It is necessary for me to drop all respect for tradition, opinion, and judgment. It is necessary for me to erase the rambling text that others have written."[17]

### Saturday 26 November

I told Mr. Leon I would drop by today and surrender my red "I am a bell ringer" smock and bell today so that someone with a better attitude could ring it during the acme of the shopping season. The drawbridge was up so I walked down one street to some President, maybe Harrison, and I was soon as lost as Moses. I retraced my steps and found the bridge, or *a* bridge—I couldn't tell anymore whether it was the same one. I couldn't make up my mind which way to go, so I walked as fast as I could in the opposite of the direction that felt right, a strategy that works slightly more than half of the time. Hurray for the God-damned idiot! Hray! Then I came to another street with a President's name: Clinton, but I decided that it wasn't *that* Clinton, so this street couldn't be or wasn't

---

[17] For erase, substitute *burn.* The same goes for Robert Rauschenberg and his *Erased de Kooning Drawings.*

necessarily parallel to the other President streets. The more I thought about it, the more parallelism lapsed into a myth no more believable to modern man than the flat earth. Every street would hit every other street if you walked fast enough and didn't panic. At the train station, I found a conductor and pretended to be from out of town so I wouldn't have to feel ashamed about asking for directions. Lying made me doubly ashamed.

"Take me, take me, web of folly and pain."
—Franz Kafka, 6 July 1916[18]

"Rape me, rape me, men of trolleys and trains."
—David Edgar Felsenstein

### Sunday 27 November

Mr. Leon ignored me at first, making me sit in the thrift shop for forty-five minutes before calling me in. "I thought you were coming yesterday, Dave. There was a kid who was going to take your place. He got a haircut and everything. This boy was neat and courteous. But without a smock and a bell he had to go home. 'What are you doing home, Johnny? I thought today you were going to collect for the Salvation Army? You're my little Soldier without a Sword.' Tears come to the boy's eyes. 'Oh, Ma, I couldn't today because they didn't have my smock and my bell.' A boy who disappoints his mother has the right to tear up. But when that boy finds out who's responsible, his eyes will be dry and narrowed."

"I apologize for my delinquency. There was an

---

[18] *Diaries* (New York: Schocken), 1948, p. 365.

unforseeable circumstance. I washed and ironed the smock, if that's okay."

Mr. Leon softened. "That was very thoughtful of you, Dave. Merry Christmas to you."

"I'm Jewish."

### Monday 28 November

I didn't want Eve to know I was reading Beckett. Nobody reads him but writers, and that's the last impression I want her to have. I made an exception this one time, but I want to retain my policy of not reading in the library. This desire is a manifestation of my not wanting to become like the Self-Taught Man of Sartre's *Nausea* (nobody reads Sartre but college boys) whose stated mission is to read every volume in the library in alphabetical order, but who actually has other things on his mind.[19]

I sat down by the magazines with *Stories and Texts for Nothing*, in a spot from which I could see her whenever I looked up from the book. For six hours she never left the counter once; she sat up straight on her stool and smiled equally at every patron. More an image of a woman in a black-and-white film than a real woman,[20] Eve shows no sign of bodily function.

---

[19] "He had set his book down in front of him but he was not reading. He was smiling at a seedy looking student who often comes to the library" (New York: New Directions, 1964), p. 38.

[20] When I say this I don't mean to detract from her beauty or her sensuality, though I am familiar with the "the case of the color-blind painter" (*New York Review of Books* [1987; 34: 25-34]), in which Oliver Sacks and Robert Wasserman detail the case of an abstract expressionist who lost his perception of color after a car accident and thereafter found his wife's flesh repulsive.

## Wednesday 30 November

Why is *disorder* a synonym for *disease*? *Time* just ran a cover story on attention deficit disorder (ADD), yet another example of the medical establishment inventing a syndrome where none exists. Future generations will gasp in dismay when they read diagnoses such as, "Patients cannot settle on a career. They cannot keep a job. They procrastinate a lot." "They sit in front of a book for 45 minutes; nothing happens."[21] *Time* publishes this kind of story so that readers, lacking religion and patriotism, can collectively identify with something, even the most chimerical of pseudoscience.[22] But not me; if I sit in front of a book for 45 minutes, you can bet your gold fillings something will happen.

Getting lost is the most flamboyant manifestation of my condition only because an intelligent person can more easily conceal mechanical ineptitude and reckless driving. They all fall under the category of narcolepsy, which, I am increasingly positive, accounts for the whole thing. River Phoenix made narcolepsy adorable in *My Own Private Idaho*, swooning with balletic poise and waking with a start, all befuddled and tousled. In reality, a silent horror pierces most episodes of narcolepsy. I perceive them as approximately suicidal moments, because they occur not when I'm curled up with a safe book but when I am at the mercy of speeding automobiles driven by myself or

---

[21] Drs. Walid Shekim and Bruce Roseman, respectively, quoted in Claudia Wallis, "Life in Overdrive," *Time* (18 July 1994): 47. Like Allen Ginsberg, "I'm obsessed by Time Magazine" ("America" [*The Portable Beat Reader* (New York: Viking, 1992), p. 75]).

[22] cf. "Genetics: The Future Is Now" cover story 17 January 1994.

others. Who has not felt the urge to succumb to the maternal embrace of three tons of speeding steel? To know the sudden taste of rent flesh salted with glass splinters? Who doesn't sometimes feel like Stendhal, who "walked the streets of Paris like a passionate dreamer, gazing at the sky and always on the point of being run over by a cab"?[23]

This is one of the many ways I expect to die: feet flying and fists pumping, I am jogging at a good clip until a commuter bus jumps the curb and knocks me skyward.

### Thursday 1 December

Earlier this evening, I was stir-frying fish heads with soy sauce and ginger, caught between the sound of Albert Ayler's "Bells" and Mrs. Bryars's. Puh-lease. No. Puh-lease. No. Puh-lease. Meanwhile, Ayler's *At Slug's Saloon* on the turntable was making me think of the day they found the saxophonist tied to a jukebox at the bottom of the East River. The liner notes say Moorish music was an influence. I don't know about that, but I can recognize the sound of unendurable joy. He had found such intense beauty that the prospect of finding it again frightened him. Coming again and again against the conclusion that the vast majority of people wouldn't or couldn't open their ears to it, he must have wondered if their failure meant he was crazy. Somewhere between "Bells" and "Ghosts," I looked toward the ceiling in irritation and realized—oops—that the ringing had stopped. And yet it was still there, like the

[23] *The Life of Henry Brulard* (Chicago: University of Chicago Press, 1958), p. 277.

feeling of a baseball cap on my head long after it has been removed.[24]

Bells command action. A bell can be a call to prayer, a call to a meal, or a call to fight. A bell is a musical instrument, but in none of these cases does the ringing qualify as music. Just as the answer to somebody at a punk rock concert in the seventies who complained, "God! They can't play!" was, "Yeah, aren't they great!"[25]—the answer to someone in the previous decade at a free jazz[26] performance who complained, "But it's not music!" was, "Thank God!"

An expert verifies, "No disaster seems to make an impression as lasting as that caused by fire."[27] I intend to create an art form from explosives, a pyrotechnic art that will take the fire out of the Independence Day sky and into the consciousness of America. "But that's not art! That's terrorism!" Thank you, thank you, thank you.

### Friday 2 December

Package from Wilmette came today, a day late. A twenty, 3 tens, 56 fives, 370 ones, 108 quarters, 80 dimes, 239 nickels, and 1,115 pennies. $708.10 Dad spent 14 dollars on postage.

---

[24] Part of the reason professional ballplayers act so childishly off the field is that they never quite shake that feeling. This is the drama of most of the dozens of baseball movies: reconciliation of their on- and off-the-diamond selves.

[25] Tom Goodkind, liner notes to *Rock at the Edge*, Arista Records, 1986.

[26] Or John Cage, or in the 1920s, George Antheil.

[27] Paul M. Angle, in his introduction to Robert Cromie's *The Great Chicago Fire* (New York: McGraw-Hill), 1958, p. ix.

## Saturday 3 December

The videos came today! *1941* is not as irreverent as I had remembered it; rather, its jokes are so bloodless and predictable that they must have been written by committee, and the result is artistically bad and plotwise anarchic enough to serve as a disciplinary exercise for my flabby mind.[28] If I force myself to watch it repeatedly, every night if necessary, I will learn concentration and lucidity.[29]

I had all my thoughts during the first screening. Had it remained on the page, *1941* could have attained the majestic giddiness of Thomas Pynchon. As a movie, its potential in this area is undermined by the dialogue and acting. Dan Aykroyd and Treat Williams shout their lines by rote; then their expressions go blank as they pause— for what? For a laugh from the audience of crew members and loved ones? For further instruction from Spielberg? Only Belushi manages to deliver his lines with aplomb. He seems borrowed from an entirely different movie.

Nevertheless, some of the situations strongly recall vintage Pynchon. The crew of a lone Japanese submarine lost in the Pacific but determined to find and attack Hollywood. Their prisoner, played of course by Slim Pickens, swallows the compass from the Crackerjack box—ingesting, in a way, his own daily allowance of

---

[28] It is the mark of a great mind to read great literature and watch wretched movies. Too many people these days try to fake their way through society by doing the opposite.

[29] The American male adolescent derives much of his power from the ability to withstand repetitive noisy nonsense. Personal stereo headphones require powerful magnets, which I suspect interact with brain cells to produce addictive compounds.

magnet. The forlorn Japs pour prune juice down his throat and wait for him to shit it out. Toilet gags that Pynchon could have stretched for pages. General Joseph W. Stillwell in a movie theater singing along with "Baby Mine" from *Dumbo* while a U.S.O. dance erupts into a riot outside.

It's hard to believe that Spielberg didn't make such a commercial failure on purpose, coming as it did four years after *Jaws* and two after *Close Encounters of the Third Kind,* and two years before *Raiders of the Lost Ark* and three before *E.T.: The Extra-Terrestrial.* Knowing it came more than a decade before Spielberg found monotheism in the story of a greedy gentile, I see the movie as a sacrifice of Belushi to the gods of commerce.

Like other greats, *Sunset Boulevard*, *Chinatown*, *Blade Runner*, *Falling Down*, it not only takes place in Los Angeles, it tells the story of Los Angeles, ground zero of the world's self-mockery. In its winkingly callous way, *1941* pokes fun at the city's troubles. "Maybe in the future, we can have some Negroes come in, and we'll have a *race* riot here," bellows the general.

Because I extracted all of the meaning and metaphor from it the first time, every subsequent viewing will seem exactly like the previous one. I won't notice new things or arrive at any fresh observations.

### Monday 5 December

Today in the library I found a marked-up copy of Nietzsche's *Beyond Good and Evil*. The vandal did not underline, as do students who expect that someday they'll have to prove that they read something, nor did he contribute marginalia, as do readers who lack the patience to just read without entering into a conversation with the author.[30] Rather, he maintained a singular purpose. He crossed out the word *not* wherever he found it, and he added it wherever he didn't, and made whatever other adjustments were necessary to reverse the meaning in the text: "The greatest thoughts are NOT the greatest events." "Every profound thinker is more afraid of being MISunderstood than of being XXXunderstood." "Now the world is NOT laughing, the dread curtain is NOT rent, the wedding day has NOT come for light and darkness." "The criminal is often enough XXX equal to his deed."

At first I despaired of this approach to reading Nietzsche, but as I turned the pages, I soon understood that this vandal was no vandal, nor was he offering a critique of the philosopher. Rather, he was *writing* a book, one that had virtually nothing to do with the original volume. The author foresaw a world darker and funnier than Nietzsche's. I turned to the title page, expecting to learn his name, but I found all the front pages had been torn out. The author of the book possessed the modesty and good taste to preserve his anonymity—that being "a condition of poetry."[31]

### Tuesday 6 December

Mrs. Bryars was lying in wait for me when I came in from the library. "Mr. Felsenstein, what good luck running into you like this."

---

[30] "How can you say that? What about Hitler?! What about Manson?!!!"; such people love exclamation points to death.

[31] John Crowe Ransom, *The World's Body* (New York: Scribner's, 1938): p. 2. Oscar Wilde said it first: "To reveal art and conceal the artist is art's aim" ("Preface to *The Picture of Dorian Gray*").

"Mrs. Bryars, you're trembling."

"I was at the mall and there was a *hostage situation*. Actually it's not a mall, it's Old Orchard, the outdoor shopping center. They're doing so much construction down there. I bought the new fruit-acid exfoliative. The skin underneath your skin is young and healthy."

"What about the hostages?"

"Just one hostage," she sighed. "An estranged girlfriend getting a perm. But he had her in there for four hours. They closed some of the shops, but the ones that remained open were mobbed. People heard about the hostage situation and they got in their cars."

"Did they shoot the terrorists?"

"There wasn't any terrorist, just a mad boy with a gun. Listen, are you very busy right now? Could I trouble you for a minute? I'm not sure whether the ringer on my phone is working. Could you dial my number, please?"

### Wednesday 7 December

*The Lord's Prayer* came in a glossy package that showed a reproduction of Matthias Grünewald's scabby altarpiece the *Crucifixion* glowing on a television screen. A sticker said that it was Number 1 in a series called "Video Seminary."

A message at the beginning of the video explains that what follows is actually a re-creation of the film *The Lord's Prayer* by Theodore (and not Salim as the catalog said) Sultan, the only surviving copy of which is in such a precarious physical state that it would not have survived the transfer to video. This dubious contention also plays at the end of the film.

The re-creation, or the film underneath the film, convincingly gives the impression of being produced on primitive film equipment, an effect that is heightened by the scratches that run the length of the film and the occasional splices. A black-clad rabbi stands just outside a white building, at the bottom of a staircase. He is wearing a fur hat and wire glasses, and his beard is streaked with gray. He holds a stack of cue cards at his side. A bicycle goes by, and a couple with a dog, but his eyes do not follow them. He faces forward and shows the cards to the camera one by one, letting each drop to the ground as he reaches for the next. The words are printed in large black lower-case letters:

our father which /art/ in heaven /hallowed be thy /name thy kingdom /come /thy will /be done on /earth as it is /in heaven give /us /this day /our daily bread /and forgive /us our debts /as we /forgive our debtors /and lead /us /not into /temptation but /deliver us /from /evil for thine /is the kingdom/ and the /power /and the /glory forever /amen

### Thursday 8 December

Shaved my head this afternoon. There was an old interview with Peter Gabriel in *Rolling Stone*[32] where he recommended that everyone should do it once. Not only did I immediately agree, I realized that I couldn't wait. I didn't have any of the right equipment, and with a pair of plastic scissors and about sixteen disposable razors, the job took hours. Too bad I didn't think to film it from beginning to end. I would title the result "Samson and Delilah" and credit myself for both roles.

---

[32] 29 January 1987.

I can't keep my hands off. My scalp is ridged and asymmetrical with a surprisingly deep indentation posterior to and to the right of the crown. The phrenologists would say that my self-esteem is pronounced and my continuity is recessed. Of the pseudosciences, phrenology resembles genetics even more than eugenics does. Eugenics intended to perfect the race, where phrenology merely nudged lucky guesses toward absolutes, which is precisely where science excels.[33]

Mrs. Bryars saw me in the parking lot and told me it was a great improvement. She ran her fingers over my naked scalp and offered to give me an emollient made from aloe, orange peel, and Vancouver moss.

"That skin isn't used to the sunlight. You should pick up some SPF-40 and take plenty of vitamin D."

"With your help, I'll live forever."

"What?" she snapped. "Nobody lives forever. We all die, and then who knows what will happen to us. The important thing is to look your best while you're alive."

---

[33] "Even Coleridge . . . thought that phrenology was 'worth some consideration' and that 'all the coincidences which have been observed could scarcely be by accident'" *The Table Talk and Omniana of Samuel Taylor Coleridge* (24 June 1827).

The situation is never as bad and always much worse than imagined by the conspiracy theorists—that species even more important to shun these days than religious zealots. A continuum of individuals, too headstrong ever to have met let alone conspired, have acted independently, leaving ruts and potholes in our intellectual history to the point where passage is near impossible. These individuals have shifted the emphasis so that, where once one group did something important, now another one does. Where once Dante built the cosmologies, now somebody named Peebles[34] does. Dante envisioned a world so complete they could map it. But a change took place in this century.[35] Now a man like Peebles runs scared from The Big Bang—if not so splendid a metaphor for creation, the only one available at the moment. "The universe we observe is inferred to be close to homogenous, with no preferred center that might have been the site of an explosion."[36] "We observe," "inferred," "close to," "might have been"—all disclaimers, in case the Big Bang turns out to be the objective truth after all, he can blame the calculator manufacturer. There are plenty of things that are superior about the modern age, and I'm glad to be here, but the cowards are everywhere, and they need lawyers like chickens need eggs.

---

[34] *Principles of Physical Cosmology* (Princeton University Press, 1993).

[35] If you believe Peter Greenaway, who says that "Heaven and hell have been cosmographically well and truly displaced" (*Flying Out of This World* (Chicago: University of Chicago Press, 1994), p. 118.

[36] Peebles, p. 6. If Peebles had written *The Divine Comedy*, he would have concluded it: "The alleged force designated arbitrarily as 'love' that moves or appears to move, depending on one's vantage point, the sun and perhaps some other stars."

"As to whether medicine was an art or a science in the Middle Ages, there can be no discussion. It was an art, pure and simple."[37] Some time after the Middle Ages, science overtook the body. Most of us wouldn't object to that, only it has done such a terrible job with it.[38] Later, with the pseudoscience of phrenology, science attempted to overtake the mind. Despite appearances, the discipline never really went away. In fact, this fanciful notion of reading bumps on the head engendered much of what is now accepted as science. "Phrenologists were not merely advertisers of evolutionary theory, they actually helped to produce it."[39] And from that clue, tracing the evolution of phrenology[40] becomes simple; it split off into psychoanalysis here and there eugenics—another supposedly discredited science that thrives today as genetics.

Neither artists nor scientists are the culprits, but pseudoscientists, whose investigations renounce both beauty and truth: Charles Darwin, who said of Shakespeare, "I found it so intolerably dull that it nauseated me,"[41] or Sigmund Freud, who drew his scientific theories from Shakespeare and then reciprocated by misapplying his pseudoscientific genius to literature.[42]

---

[37] Dean Putnam Lockwood, *Ugo Benzi* (University of Chicago Press, 1952), p. 125.

[38] "Half of their remedies cured you dead," Kipling's words on eighteenth-century medicos, apply to his own age, and to ours. This proportion must remain constant if medical technology is to go forward.

[39] David de Giustino, *Conquest of Mind* (Totowa, NJ: Rowman and Littlefield, 1975), p. 51.

[40] Or should I say the phrenology of evolution?

[41] *Autobiography*, edited by G. de Beer, 1974.

[42] Harold Bloom has found more profit in a Freudian reading of

The transformation was completed when Thomas Pynchon, the last cosmologist of the old school, wrote *Vineland*, which envisions God as a computer programmer whose creatures only matter to him as 0's or 1's, dead or alive.

Art has failed because it never assimilated the lessons of science. Most artists operate on the basis of pre-Copernican, pre-Darwinian[43] assumptions, and this has left their works cosmically invalid and biologically unstable. Meanwhile, the scientists know enough to copy the illogic and intuition of art without falling victim to its impractical Byzantinism.[44]

Art is not itself a genetic trait. Margaret Mead discovered in New Guinea that artists are born with their umbilical cords wrapped around their necks,[45] which explains the aversion to neckties and the preference for turtleneck sweaters among artists in our own culture. I don't know whether I myself was one of these newborns, but it's not too late to ask Mom.

No matter how art arises, it could still operate on

---

[42] (cont) Shakespeare than in a Shakespearean reading of Freud. For an example of Freud's misperception of the novel, see "Dostoevsky and Parricide," which blames Raskolnikov's troubles on narcolepsy. Perhaps I can employ the same defense.

[43] And yet, post-Freudian. Remember the Hasid on campus who said, "The last 150 years have seen four great thinkers: Marx, Darwin, Freud, and Einstein. Three were Jewish and one was wrong."

[44] What I mean by that is W. B. Yeats's "agony of a flame that cannot singe a sleeve" ("Byzantium," *The Collected Poems* [New York: Macmillan], 1956.)

[45] *Dedalus* (Winter 1960).

genetic principles.[46] Art must accept that its overriding purpose is the inspiration of more art.

### Saturday 10 December

Today I broke the most important rule in the library: Quiet, please. You can keep the only copy of Seneca[47] five months beyond its due date, shelve a physics text with the biographies, even drop a novel in a foul urban gully, as long as you observe silence. I should have gone to the bank first and then the library, or at least kept the coins in a stronger bag. The canvas Harold Washington Library bag was showing signs of wear, but I didn't pay attention. The seam split, the coins spilt. A thunder of metal and marble floor, an explosion in the library. I'm just glad that Eve wasn't there to witness my folly. The scatter of coins was at once a physics lesson, a musical number, and an art project.

A guard came over to help me with the coins.

"It's okay," I said. "I got it."

"It's my responsibility to help you with these. These are evidence."

I think I said, "Wah?"

"Evidence against you. For the crime of robbing our fountain."

"The bag broke. These were my—"

"You took these coins out of our fountain. All those kids making a wish won't get their wishes now."

---

[46] Just as "a gene might be able to assist replicas of itself which are sitting in other bodies." Richard Dawkins, *The Selfish Gene* (New York: Oxford University Press, 1976), p. 95. Dawkins gives albinism as an example.

[47] "With afflictions of the spirit, . . . the worse a person is, the less he feels it" (*Letters from a Stoic* [New York: Penguin, 1969], LIII, 6).

"I need a lawyer."

Laughter. Echoing laughter, and a warm smile. "I'm playing. I'm in the library all day. Kind of like you, except they pay me for it. My name is Silas." His name tag said S. Dowdell. His face was black, his lips so red he'd leave marks wherever he kissed. We shook hands.

"Thanks for the help," I said. "Look at all this."

"Yeah, I could see how you could live here. Find a little spot where security can't find you. Eat our candy bars. Wash in our sink. Collect money from our fountain. Like those kids in the book who lived in the Metropolitan Museum of Art."

"What book?"

"*From the Mixed-Up Files of Mrs. Basil E. Frankweiler.* Never read that one?"

"No," I tried to smile. "Reading isn't really my thing."

### Sunday 11 December

Because of all the confusion yesterday, I walked out of the library without remembering to look for something by Empedocles, the philosopher who jumped into a volcano in order to prove he was a god. Now that has to wait until tomorrow. Too bad I don't live in the library.

### Monday 12 December

This morning I bought a Cubs hat and a lipstick-red, 1,000 gauss[48] horseshoe magnet, which rested snugly

---

[48] Named for Friedrich Carl Gauss (1777-1855) (Siddhartha Gautama comes right after him in *Webster's New Biographical Dictionary*), who viewed the development of a theory of magnetism as an aesthetic project. Frederick Engels derides his

in my scalp indentation—a necessary complement to the fish head diet for training my sense of direction. The ends point forward, creating something that resembles the *Moses* of Michelangelo, which is why I needed the hat. Attuned to whatever minuscule changes in circulation and brain wavelength that may have been taking place, I walked straight up Clark, the crooked spine of a crooked city.

Although I knew that people couldn't see what I had under my hat, I couldn't help feeling they knew I was up to no good. I had difficulty affecting the manner of the flaneur, strolling and looking in shop windows, and not just a plain wandering (lost) Jew. With this in mind, I deliberately bought some *traif* near Belmont Avenue. "Hello, sport, it's good to see you again," said the man behind the counter, possibly a Greek. When he saw that I looked perplexed, he added, "I apologize, sir. It's my head. Last week I was walking with my son and I wasn't looking where I was going and I walked wham straight into a pole. When they picked me up from the street I didn't know nobody no more. The doctors say it will come back, but meantime I say hello to people like I know them. I'm trying to run a business."

Chewing thoughtfully on my Polish, I accepted the story without comment, but then a man appeared behind

---

48 (con't) "mathematical mysticism" (in his *Anti-Duhring*), though Gauss's biographer claims, "He was distrustful of mystical short-cuts (the trap of 'professional' romantic poets and philosophers)" (W. K. Buhler, *Gauss* [Berlin: Springer, 1981], p. 65). Also: "Gauss's brain, with its, as it turns out, exceptionally deep and numerous convolutions, has been incorporated in the anatomical collection of the University of Göttingen" (p. 155). Probably a result of his messing around with magnets.

me, younger than the owner and apparently overflowing with an urgent rebuttal. He led me away from the counter and, struggling to determine the best place to begin the story, clapped his hands once in mute rage. He blinked his eyes and asked for a sip of my drink. Finally, he smiled. "That's all true," he said, "except I was the one who walked into the post. I bumped my head. I saw stars. I got a lump, but I'm fine. Now my dad has amnesia."

### Tuesday 13 December

Early in the century, while Lenin planned revolution and Joyce planned *Ulysses* in Zurich, Hugo Ball and his dadaist friends were across town fighting their own wars. During his life and in his writing, Hugo Ball violated every religious code he could think of, but he embraced the Church before he died, and his wife Emmy Hennings made sure that all of his anti-Catholic writings were destroyed.[49]

None of the accounts of that time mention anything about films being shown at the Cabaret Voltaire. I doubt the equipment to do so would have been mobile or affordable enough. The reference in the video catalog to Richard Huelsenbeck destroying *The Lord's Prayer* might have resulted from a misinterpretation of an event he records in his memoirs, a stampede in a cinema during the summer of 1916 so chaotic that he lost his girlfriend L—— in the confusion and never saw her again. He neglects to mention what film was being shown at the time.

I found no reference to either Salim or Theodore Sultan in any index of the histories of Dada. Hans Richter—a

---

[49] She wrote a book called *Hugo Ball's Road to God.*

man Huelsenbeck called "the greatest moralist among the dadaists"[50]—produced some films, but according to their descriptions none have the elegant spareness of *The Lord's Prayer.*

### Wednesday 14 December

While walking today I spotted Eve across the street, and I began following her—a challenge because she walks slowly, looking down at the pavement, brushing against the sides of buildings, and I tend to walk speedily. But I have followed women before, and I know the many strategies.[51] Her long coat had a fur collar, and the right shoulder was blackened with grime from being brushed alongside buildings. Eve rolls like a stream, eroding the edges of the city. Hypnotic clutching and tensing of the muscle, under successive layers of flesh, cotton, wool, satin, and cashmere.

She stopped once to lean against a concrete planter on State Street, and at first I thought she knew she was being pursued, but then I figured out that she was stopping to catch her breath. She is only a fragile thing.

I hadn't been thinking about where she was going; I suppose that I was entertaining a vague notion of following her onto a bus, getting off at her stop and offering

---

[50] Huelsenbeck, *Memoirs of a Dada Drummer* (New York: Viking, 1974), p. 107.

[51] "To follow the other," writes Jean Baudrillard, "is to take charge of [her] itinerary; it is to watch over [her] life without [her] knowing it; it is to relieve [her] of that existential burden, the responsibility for [her] own life" (text from the back cover of Sophie Calle's *Suite Vénitienne: Please Follow Me* [Seattle: Bay Press, 1983]). You've got to love a writer who gets it so totally wrong.

# How to Study Shaftesbury's Personal Magnetism Books

E hope to complete a READING GUIDE to the study of Shaftesbury's Magnetism Books, and will send you one as soon as it is completed. In the meantime the following suggestions will prove helpful. The plan here presented will prevent you feeling that you "don't know where to begin" or "can't make head nor tail of it."

*First*—The lessons entitled "Cultivation of Personal Magnetism" (otherwise known as the Exercises of the Personal Magnetism Club)—are the FOUNDATION of the magnetism system as a whole. Probably you are either receiving those lessons now as part of the set—or as thousands have done, you are one who had those lessons prior to receiving these other large volumes.

*Either way*—we assume you have read "Cultivation of Personal Magnetism" or have it here now and will start with that first. That is the only book of exercises in the whole great system. But such exercises and tests are essential to generate and store vital magnetic power within the brain and body. The other books show you how to brilliantly USE such powers.

*Each division*—"Mental, Advanced, Sex Magnetism," etc., is a complete study unit in itself. No one book actually depends upon any other in order to give you new powers and benefits that are far reaching in their value and help. But ALL of the advanced lessons yield better results if you have first laid the solid foundation of personal magnetic power by an earnest study of "Cultivation of Personal Magnetism."

After the foundation book, we suggest "MENTAL MAGNETISM" as an easy and delightful start. This is the magnetism of the Brain—the field of mastery over the thoughts. It aims to give you skill and strategy in all the mental conflicts of life. Read into the system as time and inclination permit.

Next we suggest either SEX Magnetism or the OTHER MIND. Neither of these will prove difficult, but each will grip your interest and hold your attention and continually reveal some new idea, help, value.

Then UNIVERSAL Magnetism should be started—taking it slowly. While this is Shaftesbury's highest and most exalted

to carry her bag, being invited up to her efficiency, and talking until dawn about the library system in America. "Yes, David, that's a refreshing insight about the electronic card catalog—and quite honestly it makes me feel much better about my job. Now, tell me about yourself." I pictured Eve lit by candles of unusual colors. I imagined us sitting on the floor, drinking tea, talking and talking and then falling into a long silence.

Actually, I thought we were heading north on State, but about a block from the library I finally realized that she was going to work, not coming from it. I nearly followed her in, but I had no pencil, and I hate those little miniature-golf pencils they have in there. This turned out to be a lucky decision, because when I got home—two hours and fifty blocks later—I discovered that the wind had blown my Cubs hat off my head and that I had been walking downtown like that—a bald guy with a magnet on his head. Medium height, medium build.

### Thursday 15 December

No. 6 of six significant characteristics of individuals who are potential problem sleepers: "Socially fearful . . . asking someone the simplest direct questions can be embarrassing and extremely difficult. . . . One 25-year-old man walked over 100 city blocks to his destination because he was too embarrassed to ask a train conductor for directions."[52]

No. 14 of twenty "Peculiar Cases Treated by Dr. R. S. Thacker of Delhi": "*Mental Sickness*—Sardar, B.S. (27

---

[52] Henry Kellerman, *Sleep Disorders: Insomnia and Narcolepsy* (New York: Brunner/Mazel), 1981, pp. 18-19.

years) could not do any mental work. He preferred to remain silent, talked rarely and became unconscious sometimes. He took magnetic treatment for about 6 months and drank magnetised water during the whole treatment. He became not only normal but overactive and is now running his business successfully."[53]

## Friday December 16

A flag flapping in the breeze upholds the triumph of property, while a flag in flames embodies the potential of art, but only the potential. This applies to the American flag, the most didactic of national emblems, more than the swastika. That is, the swastika imparts no lesson, while the American flag goes on and on like a great uncle.

After dreaming of the American flag in 1954, Jasper Johns began painting it, laying stripe after stripe until the creation became a kind of destruction. He painted old glory with the wrong number of stripes, painted it green, drained it of color until it was a flag of surrender. He pinned it down flat so that it could not ripple. He dragged it into the museums, where the ceilings are too low for it;

---

[53] H. L. Bansal, *Magnetotherapy* (New Delhi: B. Jain, 1976): p. 119. The library has many volumes on this subject, including Ralph U. Sierra's *Power in a Magnet* (the title of which comes from the quotation, "There is power in a magnet," spoken by Paracelsus [1493-1541], the discoverer of magnetotherapy), H. H. Sherwood's *Manual for Magnetizing*, and James V. Wilson's *How to Magnetize*. Samuel Hahnemann and Franz Mesmer (from whom the term *mesmerize* comes) practiced advanced magnetotherapy in the late eighteenth century. During the next century it was employed mainly in cases of hysteria. Doctors applied magnets to the head and uterus.

hanging there at half mast, it imposes a perpetual state of grief on the nation. But when people stopped going to museums, the flags turned back into paintings.

In the next decade, they started burning flags, which they wouldn't have done without Jasper Johns. The State incited counterrevolution among the middle-class and passed blatantly unconstitutional laws to stop it, but there was never any real cause for alarm. The revolution fell short, but not because of the State. The flag burners mishandled their gesture in two ways. First, they burned flags for a specific political and historical purpose. Fire, like art, is always diminished by an agenda. Second, they allowed their actions to be reduced to the condition of the theater. The capitol steps are no place for art.

### Saturday 17 December

"We do not imagine Dante or Shakespeare keeping track of the trifling incidents of their lives in order to bring them to other people's attention."[54] If I cannot resist keeping this notebook, I must at least keep the trivia out of it, because it already has a higher purpose. The wrong words could endanger lives and property. The right words might still wreak havoc. Either way, the notebook gets burned. The pen gets drowned in the river.

What counts as trivia? Love, lust, food, money, fashion, entertainment, architecture, politics, newspapers, television, sports, death, disease, technology, friendship, the environment, race, class, education, family, and children.

---

[54] E. M. Cioran, *The Temptation to Exist,* translated by Richard Howard (Chicago: Quadrangle Books, 1968), p. 136.

All these things will be abandoned with the passage of time. With our Prozac, attorneys, and David Letterman,[55] we are living through the era of collateral damage.

## Sunday 18 December

The falling snow made the air very dry tonight, and the flag burned very nicely. I nearly set fire to one in front of a barbershop on the West Side, but I heard a phone ringing above me and got scared that somebody would come to the window. I found a better one in front of a quiet house in the neighborhood. It hung down low enough that I could spritz it with gasoline and touch a burning matchbook to it when there was nobody in sight, and I watched it burn from a safe distance. There was a feeling of pride in the sight, not at all the anarchic pride that I had expected, but rather an emotion that I sheepishly recognized as patriotism. As they climbed, the flames brightened the colored threads, sparks fluttered to the ground, and I felt sure that a fife-and-drum corps would come marching along at any moment to run the charred remains up a pole.

## Monday 19 December

Today in the library in the third-floor men's bathroom, I discovered a little turd, about the size and shape of a squash ball, in the first urinal on the left. It was nearly black against the bubble-gum pink of the urinal cake.

---

[55] It has been said that Walt Whitman "bears a relation to Lincoln not unlike Shakespeare's to Elizabeth I and Michelangelo's to the Medici" (Howard Moss, *Minor Monuments* [New York: The Ecco Press, 1986], p. 107), and I think that goes for Letterman and Bill Clinton, too.

"You might not want to hear this," I said to Eve as I handed her de Kruif's *Microbe Hunters*.

"Oh-oh. What is it? Nails on a chalkboard? The grinding a car makes when you try to start it after it's already on? Teenagers kissing at the movies? Boot heel on a cat's tail?"

"What's the loudest sound the ear can stand without sustaining damage?" I asked, deciding to forget about the condition of the men's room.

"130 decibels is the average level for pain. I'd say 140 would do some damage. Good luck and have a nice day."

I permitted myself to rest my eyes on her right ear for a few seconds before I turned away.

## Tuesday 20 December

The Buddhists are coming! The library newsletter announced that eight Tibetan monks from the Ganden Monastery, built in Lhasa in 1409, will spend March 1-4 constructing a sand mandala on the ground floor.

"The mandala is a religious symbol unique to Tibetan Buddhism. Mandala means 'circle' and represents the universe. Comprised of a series of concentric circles, the multi-colored intricate sand paintings depict Tantric deities.

"With a cone-shaped, fine-tipped funnel, Tibetan artists have been able to make these amazingly complex and vivid sand mandalas from a rich and diverse palate.

"They believe that the mandala is healing to the spectator and abetting of concentration for the practitioner.

"Tibetans revere the sand mandala as a sacred object, but it is not intended to endure long. Upon its consecration the colored sands of the mandala are swept up and then poured into a nearby river, lake, or ocean. The idea being that these waters carry the tiny blessed particles throughout the environment, conferring everywhere a purifying influence."[56]

The Navajo Indians use sand paintings as a healing ritual. Jackson Pollock acknowledged that his method of painting copied theirs. Like the Tibetans, the Navajos color sand with natural products. The charred root of the rock oak when mixed with white sand makes a pastel blue. The Navajo chief Hosteen Klah presented the art at the Century of Progress world fair in Chicago in 1934. President Franklin Delano Roosevelt signed his name in the register of the hall where the sand painting was on display. Hosteen Klah visited the Adler Planetarium and saw the Milky Way through its enormous telescope.

### Wednesday December 21

Robert Rauschenberg threw his paintings in the river after exhibiting them. John Cage asked, "What is the nature of Art when it reaches the Sea?"[57]

### Thursday December 22

Today I torched the barber's flag. I got away clean, but I thought I heard sirens behind me. Wearing the magnet as an amulet of invisibility, I walked in a six-block-radius circle around the barbershop, and when I returned I saw

---

[56] *Library Line* (January-March 1995).

[57] Cage, *Silence* (Middleton, CT: Wesleyan University Press, 1961), p. 98.

something that I thought was a corpse slumped out of the window above the flagpole. The smoke had left a black mark on the pale brick wall.

### Friday December 23

I'm giddy and inflamed, yet also troubled by the visitation of the monks. The library could have a deadening impact on their magic sand crystals. The place accommodates me so well largely because it houses dead things without allowing them to decompose. I am with Jorge Luis Borges, who "imagined Paradise as a kind of library."[58] I imagine this is the appeal of museums, art galleries, and cinemas.

Once, an artist brought 2 million live army ants into a Manhattan art gallery and displayed them in a huge plastic cube filled with sand.[59] Every single ant died before the week was over. Moral: Art laminates life.

### Saturday 24 December

Still another week to go in the month, and I'm down to pennies and nickels. Around $80 total. No one pays enough attention to pennies and nickels even to form opinions about them, even though everyone handles a few

---

[58] Borges, "Blindness," in his *Seven Nights,* translated by Eliot Weinberger, New Directions, 1980. Libraries have always been storehouses of obsolete knowledge. Now, with all the digital technologies, the library itself is becoming obsolete. Death within death, like the man who drank poison to get rid of his worms.

[59] Lewis Thomas celebrated the piece as "an abstraction, a live mobile, an action painting, a piece of found art, a happening, a parody, depending on the light" (*The Lives of a Cell* [New York: Bantam, 1975], p. 65).

of each every day. As nitrogen suspends oxygen and carbon dioxide in the atmosphere, small coins suspend the important coins and bills in the monetary flow.

Thanks to my father, who told me three years ago to "develop an intimacy with money, David, please,"[60] I handle large quantities of pennies and nickels on a constant basis and have solidified my opinions toward them. Pennies menace me. Abraham Lincoln's face strikes me as untrustworthy. He espoused the reverse of my every political instinct. As President, Lincoln instituted repression and terror within national borders.[61] Just when anarchy and fragmentation were showing signs of vitality, he killed in the name of unity and wholeness. The smell of copper on my fingers nauseates me, and I avoid foods with high concentrations of the metal.[62]

Where Lincoln faces right, his eyes on fascism, Jefferson faces to the left. On the nickel he appears humane and serene. Jefferson encouraged revolution and, when he successfully won independence from Britain, he fought to keep the United States government from repeating British mistakes.[63] His politics echo those of the

---

[60] David Edgar Felsenstein: Invest in greed, Dad? False!

[61] The *Encyclopedia Britannica* concedes, "Lincoln at times authorized his generals to make arbitrary arrests. . . . He let his generals suspend several newspapers" (Chicago: University of Chicago Press, 1973), s.v. Lincoln.

[62] "Calves' liver, chocolate, nuts, oysters and other shellfish, and dried fruits," according to Charles A. Owen, Jr., in his *Biological Aspects of Copper* (Park Ridge, NJ: Noyes, 1982), p. 7.

[63] He looked to the native tribes for political ideals and found that "those societies (as the Indians) which live without government enjoy in their general mass an infinitely greater degree of happiness than those who live under European governments" (Letter

Buddha.[64] Jefferson loved books, and his library at Monticello became the foundation for the Library of Congress. Nickel has no odor and in its purest form (e.g., in Canadian nickels) is attractive to magnets. Furthermore, "several studies in the late 1800s reported potential therapeutic uses of nickel compounds in humans."[65]

### Sunday 25 December

"From this day on, the church bell sounded to him like the voice of the angel, calling the child to him."
> —Emmy Hennings, Foreword to the 1946 edition of Hugo Ball's *Flight Out of Time*

"In what way do chimes remind you of singing?"
> —Gertrude Stein, *Accents in Alsace*

"So I wait, jogging along, for the bell to say, 'Molloy, one last effort, it's the end.'"
> —Samuel Beckett, *Molloy*

"Let the night come on bells."
> —Guillaume Apollinaire

---

63 (con't) to Edmund Carrington, 17 January 1787, published in *The Papers of Thomas Jefferson* 11:49 [Princeton: Princeton University Press, 1950-1982]).

64 Piyasena Dissanayake, in his *Political Thoughts of the Buddha,* forecasts, "The need for government will cease to exist if and when the people become free from these evils [of greed, pride, and private property]" (Colombo, Sri Lanka: Dept. of Cultural Affairs, 1977), p. 79.

65 Robert P. Hausinger, *Biochemistry of Nickel* (New York: Plenum, 1993), p. 3.

"The little bell is pulled by a rope and goes: ding, ding, ding, ding, ding."
—Wassily Kandinsky, *Sounds*, 1912, p. 38.

"The tintinnabulation that so musically wells / From the bells, bells, bells, bells."
—Edgar Allan Poe, *The Bells* (1849)

"When I hear the bells of madness ring, I will listen to the silence."
—Brian Wilson

"There were bells / on a hill / but I never heard them ringing / no, I never heard them at all."
—Meredith Willson, sung by Paul McCartney on *Meet the Beatles*

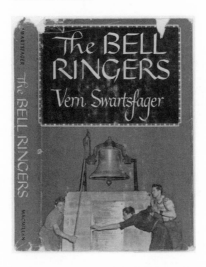

"The toll of Jetavana's temple bell echoes the transience of all earthly things; the hue of the blossoms on the *sala*

trees displays the truth that those who flourish must surely fall.

—*Tales of the House of Taira.*

"Oh, noisy bells, be dumb."
—A. E. Housman, "Bredon Hill"

"Silence that dreadful bell!"
—Shakespeare, *Othello*

"In my day, the bells no longer swung."
—Kurt Vonnegut, *Hocus Pocus*

"In early times, bells used to be consecrated with the blood of a sacrificial animal, and then struck with a wooden staff. There are several reports of bells being cast from weapons which had been taken by force or confiscated in order to nip a rebellion in the bud. It is a Buddhist custom to sound a temple bell at midnight and on the occasion of the death of a high official. No two bells sound exactly alike: some are harbingers of good fortune, some of bad.

"Bells sound particularly sweet-toned if a young girl has jumped or been thrown into the molten metal. . . . 'Burmese bells' (*mian ling*) are tiny silver bells containing tiny gold beads or grains of sand, which are inserted in the vagina or the foreskin as sexual excitants."

—Wolfram Eberhard, *A Dictionary of Chinese Symbols*

"The whorehouse bells were ringing/ And the pimp stood in the door/ He'd had a hard on all day long/ To screw some dirty whore."

—cowboy song

"Every time you hear a bell ring, it means that some angel's just got his wings."

> —Clarence (Henry Thomas) in Frank Capra's *It's a Wonderful Life* (1946)

### Monday 26 December

For the hundreds if not thousands of times she has assisted me, Eve has never once commented on the books I've checked out. I know she's interested in the titles. I saved the September-December 1988 issue of *Library Line*, which announced that she'd joined the library staff. "Ms. Jablom was graduated from Princeton University, where she earned a dual degree in math and Eastern religion before taking her master's degree in Library Science. She collects candles and devotional objects."

In the margin of the newsletter I wrote, "Eve Jablom: Jab me, Love."

Today as I checked out an armload of books on subjects related to Tibetan Buddhist thought,[66] she could have said something, voiced an objection to one volume or pointed out an insightful passage in another. She could have asked whether I knew about the coming visitation from the monks. Instead, as I gathered my books, she said: "Hair's growing in."

"I wanted to see what my scalp looked like."

---

[66] Tantrism, Mahayana Buddhism, Mandalas, Lamaism, Kashmir, etc. Both of the library's copies of Volume I of Sir John Woodroffe's (pseud. Arthur Avalon) two-volume *Principles of Tantra* (1914) are missing, as is Violet Crispe's translation of Nicolas Notovich's *On the Life of Saint Issa* (1895), which purports to be an account of Jesus Christ's teenage years in Nepal.

"Once," she remembered, "I wanted to see what my skull looked like. I asked a radiologist's assistant and she got me an appointment. But then once I had it, I lost all interest. It looked just like a skull. I ended up giving it to my mom for Christmas." She took off her wristwatch and massaged the red indentation left by the clasp. I exited and walked down Van Buren without buttoning my jacket, overheated with thoughts of the same sort of mark left by the elastic band of her underpants. When I got to Wells, I turned the wrong way and ended up at Goldberg's River City apartments. The river smelled exactly like a battery.

Which gave me the idea of keeping a 12-volt battery in my bag, attached to foil or electrodes, something to turn my whole body into an electromagnet. Directional sense isn't in the brain, it's in the spinal fluid.

### Tuesday 27 December

More than twenty screenings of *1941* were necessary before I noticed a great dadaist moment; at the start of the final scene, the sun rises over the Pacific. I will have to reevaluate my opinion of this movie.

### Wednesday 28 December

To walk in the door you would have had to pass under one wide white stripe. The immense flag, hanging right-side-down, covered most of the façade of the church. I waited as two teenage girls lingered in the parking lot. They were singing Aretha Franklin's "Think" and pointing at each other and bobbing their heads, pretending they were black. One of the girls didn't have a coat; her throat was exposed to the freezing air, and she was trying to hug herself and point at the same time. They tried to light cigarettes, but the wind kept blowing out their matches; I wanted to step out of the shadows and offer to help, but I stayed put. A van drove up and took them both away, and once it was out of sight, I stood before the flag. The only light was from the street across the churchyard, and the colors of the flag were dull.

The bigger a flag is, the less concentrated is its power, like a target that anyone could hit.

I sprayed gasoline all along the lower edge—normally the right edge—of the flag and flicked the Bic. I stood there watching it burn, until the heat reached my face. When I got home I had to throw my clothes away in the trashcan behind the building because they smelled like smoke.

### Thursday 29 December

When blues dadaist Jimi Hendrix played "The Star-Spangled Banner" at Woodstock, he did with a banner of music what the students were doing to the one of cloth, but the jingoistic tune arose from its own ashes, and Hendrix's version itself was exploited in advertising to evoke a certain kind of nostalgic, fought-for patriotism.

*Mona Lisa* fulfills a similar symbolic function, and every anti-art artist has had to take his turn trying to destroy her. Marcel Duchamp drew a mustache on her.[67] Robert

---

[67] Salvador Dali called it an act of "ultra-intellectual aggression" (*Art News* [1963; reprinted November 1992]: p. 166), and repeated it.

Rauschenberg painted the *Pneumonia Lisa*. Andy Warhol made *Thirty Are Better Than One*, repeating it over and over again in the same picture, as though trying to slice an earthworm into thirty pieces to see if any of them keep moving.

Jean Tinguely, who realized that "the polar opposite of repetition is destruction,"[68] once contemplated throwing a hand grenade at the Mona Lisa. Nothing in the books says why he didn't go through with it, but in his failure of nerve he brings to mind Mr. Vladmir in Conrad's novel, who felt "a bomb in the National Gallery would make some noise. But it would not be serious enough."[69] If a painting is despised, it is made the object of satire, or it is taken down from the wall and shelved in the attic, or it is painted over, or unkind words are written about it. We are not used to seeing burning pictures, though we do expect to see burning flags. As to why flags are not regarded as visual icons, that is the subject probed by Jasper Johns.

Do we fear visible things too much to burn them, whereas books on fire are a familiar, even a comforting sight?[70] Or do we not respect visible things enough to bother setting them on fire?

---

[68] Pontus Hulten, *Jean Tinguely: A Magic Stronger than Death* (Milan: Bompiani, 1989), p. 68.

[69] *The Secret Agent* (Middlesex: Penguin English Library, 1963), p. 67.

[70] "Let us gather some good books about the fire," as it says on the bookplate designed by William Fowler Hopson for the novelist and bibliophile John S. Wood.

## Friday 30 December

Siddhartha Gautama, the Buddha, said, "All things are on fire."[71] When I burn flags I try to think of it as creating a burning flag, not destroying the flag. The *nir tamid*, the eternal flame of the Jewish tradition.

I have tried to cultivate an indifference toward the flag, but I feel repulsion when I see it and satisfaction when it's gone. With this attitude I am likely to grow foolhardy in my plots to set flags on fire, taking bigger risks to burn bigger and more salient flags, and when caught I will be publicly mocked, and the media will make me into a minor celebrity outlaw; *Time* and *Newsweek* will seize the chance to put an image of Old Glory on their covers, and more flags than ever will fly in this city.

On the sixth day of the sixth month in 1966,[72] Sidney Street heard on the radio that a sniper in Mississippi had murdered the Civil Rights leader James Meredith. Street owned a 48-star American flag, and he brought it out to the corner of St. James Place and Lafayette Avenue in Brooklyn, held a burning match to it, and let it drop to the sidewalk. As it burned, a small crowd gathered, and Street announced to them, "If they did that to Meredith, we don't need an American flag."

Street may have burned it up, but our flag was still there. The American flag, the abstraction, thrives when one material American flag is burned. Each flag is a head of the hydra.

---

[71] Quoted in Karl Jaspers, *Socrates, Buddha, Confucius, Jesus* (San Diego: HBJ, 1962), p. 28.

[72] "Street v. New York," Robinson and Simoni, pp. 576 ff. Probably no significance should be attached to this date. Numerology is one of the very few things I don't believe in.

Joan of Arc would now be a long-forgotten precocious teen if the French had just slit her white throat in Rouen. Jimi Hendrix sanctified his instrument when he poured lighter fluid on his guitar and set it on fire at the Monterey Pop Festival during his performance of "Wild Thing." No books in history are considered to be more invested with the wisdom of mankind than the books destroyed by Omar the Caliph, who burned down the Library of Alexandria in 650 A.D.[73]

### Saturday 31 December

I would have liked to ask Eve to attend a New Year's ball with me tonight—I could present her with a corsage and she could wear a gown that leaves her shoulders exposed;[74] champagne bubbles could tickle my nose as I drank from her shoe, the heel of which could break, so that as she walked her black stockings would skim like a whisper over marble floors. I think about her every minute but cannot form a visual image of her unless I've looked at her in the previous hour. When I'm at her counter, when I should concentrate on committing her every detail to my long-term memory, my breath becomes shallow, depriving my brain of oxygen as I look through her features to imagine

---

[73] This feeling endures despite Edward Gibbon's protestations: "Nor can it fairly be presumed," he writes in volume 6 of *Decline and Fall of the Roman Empire*, "that any important truth, any useful discovery in art or nature, has been snatched away from the curiosity of modern ages."

[74] "The coraco-clavicular ligament serves to connect the clavicle with the coracoid process of the scapula" Henry Gray, F.R.S., *Anatomy: Descriptive and Surgical*. A revised American, from the 15th English, Ed. (New York: Bounty, 1978), p. 249.

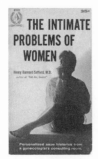

**THE INTIMATE PROBLEMS OF WOMEN**

Henry Harvard Safford, M.D.
author of "Tell Me, Doctor"

Personalized case histories from
a gynecologist's consulting room.

her snatch glowing pink through her wool A-line skirt, but I walk away, and her ovoidal face, the scent of book-binding glue that hovers around her body, and her light-brown hair and eyes slip my mind, no matter how much I attempt to memorize them. All I have is the black-and-white photo-graph from the newsletter, and that does nothing to stimulate me when I am here alone. The standard pornography does little more. It's more exciting as kindling. Only with the aid of the accurate line drawings and factual prose in *Gray's Anatomy* can I successfully trick out an erection and fabricate what it would be like to probe her ear with my finger. The auricle's "outer surface is irreg-ularly concave, directed slightly forward, and presents numerous eminences and depressions which result from the foldings of its fibro-cartilaginous element."[75]

I look forward to a time when I can look back at my short yet inauspicious career and say, with sad egolessness, "I am in retirement from love."[76] I wish I could conceal "the unhappiness of the bachelor. . . so easily guessed at by the world around him. . . . Everyone knows his condi-tion, can detail his sufferings."[77] I would like to forget Eve Jablom altogether, but how can I when, there she is, in the library, the place where I go?

A promiscuous composer said, "Unhad love is

---

[75] *Gray's Anatomy*, p. 849. God, I love that *slightly*.

[76] William Gass, *In the Heart of the Heart of the Country* (New York: Harper & Row, 1958), p. 173.

[77] Franz Kafka, *Diaries,* p. 130.

sweeter,"[78] but he didn't say that about sex. Artists demand and deserve a steady flow of the stuff. The joining of bodies shatters perspective and distorts facial features. Abundant sex, missionary style, is directly responsible for Picasso's invention of figurative cubism, where the eyes of those whores *The Demoiselles d'Avignon* swell and come together like two sausage links.

If I do destroy the library, I will be doing it for Eve, not as a desperate measure of a spurned lover, but as a work of art created for and about the loved one, like Dante's *Paradiso* or the Motown catalog. A love song with no words and no melody—just a rhythm[79] of a single beat echoing, then a long silence.

### Sunday 1 January 1995

"All bodies try to form themselves into perfect magnets,"[80] but then what? The passage into entropy, the neutralization of feeling: the color brown, where all the colors mix irretrievably together. I am making no resolution to initiate personal contact with Eve Jablom outside the library, hatching no schemes to entrap her little heart. I prefer the attraction to pull in only one direction. Mutual feelings result in "the decomposition inherent in all closed circuits."[81]

---

[78] Ned Rorem, *The Paris and New York Diaries*. San Francisco: North Point Press, 1983, p. 91.

[79] "Rhythm alone creates music, that is, what our culture recognizes in music" (Morse Peckham, *Man's Rage for Chaos* [Philadelphia: Chilton, 1965], p. 190).

[80] G. G. Zerffi, *Spiritualism and Animal Magnetism* (London: Robert Hardwicke, 1871).

[81] Jean Dubuffet, *Asphyxiating Culture* (New York: Four Walls Eight Windows, 1988), p. 99.

Creative energy flows untapped from unrequited love. Two pair of eyes cannot study each other simultaneously. The one pair sees the world, the other pair studies the eyes that see, making note of the curve of a lash, the purity and luster of the white, the fast or slow blink. This prolonged attention to the phantasmagoric play of surface builds and builds until the time comes when a powerful balance of heartbreak is there to be cashed in. The ways of cashing in are manifold, but three of the most popular are destruction, suicide, and art. My way covers those three.

### Monday 2 January

Package from Wilmette came today, since there was no mail yesterday. $719, including over four thousand pennies. Numismatic bastards, each one carries germs from a different person. They start out brave and shiny, but, like Frost says, nothing gold can stay,[82] and they end their careers the dark brown of a stool sample. Every roll of pennies a perfectly cylindrical shit sheathed in thick purple parchment.

Eventually I will burn this book, too, but until then I don't want to have to rip any pages from it. Not telling lies isn't enough. I must fulfill its promises. Writing is the easy part.

### Tuesday 3 January

"In the eighties, it was money. In the nineties, it's still money, but it's also Buddhism.[83]

---

[82] Smart man. He also says, "I hold with those who favor fire."

[83] *The New Yorker* (10 January 1994): p. 28.

"Americans live in the many worlds of a shattered culture, and, as Buddhism allows paradox, it helps to heal that shattering and grow something larger."[84]

"Buddhism is hot these days."[85]

America is at the perfect stage for a Buddhist overthrow, thanks to the economic triumph of Japan. In the 1950s, the Beat Generation authors who tried to promote Buddhism failed out of guilt for blowing up two of Japan's cities.[86] Things have changed; now that the Japanese own Manhattan as well as most of the entertainment and news media, Buddhism makes sense as a management philosophy.

Moreover, the universality of television reruns and paper and plastic recycling help us accept that a human life, too, when over, can be broken down, processed, repackaged, and resold as new.[87] Most of all, automobiles and the values they instill make Buddhism much more viable than anything in the Judeo-Christian heritage. First, Americans had love affairs with their cars. Now they have entered a new stage, one that affords a perfect analogy for the Buddhist doctrine of reincarnation: The car is to the

---

[84] Natalie Goldberg, quoted in *Publishers Weekly* (August 15, 1994): 38.

[85] Helen Cordes, "Buddhism: American Style," *The Utne Reader* (January-February 1995): p. 16. You think it's hot now, wait until I get through with it.

[86] "Go fuck yourself with your atom bomb," writes Ginsberg in "America." "I won't say the Lord's Prayer / I have mystic visions and cosmic vibrations."

[87] Like St. Augustine, we will not fear "that the omnipotence of God cannot recall all the particles that have been consumed by fire or by beasts, or dissolved into dust and ashes, or decomposed into water, or evaporated into air" (*The City of God*, xxii). Only instead of God, we have technology.

driver as the body is to the soul.[88] Americans worry about being alienated from their cars the same way they worry about being alienated from their bodies, when in both cases they should be trying to escape.

The joke is making the rounds. A moving van backs into a parked Cadillac, and seconds later a lawyer rushes out into the street, screaming "Whiplash! Whiplash!"

An American will go through many automobiles during his career as a driver. Finding one that feels right, he babies it, invites his neighbors to gawk and whistle. But then maybe he finds himself changed, and a new car is in order, even though the same driver holds the wheel.

Erwin Panofsky said in 1939, "The man who is run over by an automobile is run over by mathematics, physics and chemistry."[89] Today, we would have to maintain that he is run over by dharma, satori, and nirvana.

### Wednesday 4 January

Today in the library I took down a copy of *With a Quiet Heart*, the autobiography of the lesbian alcoholic Communist actress Eva Le Gallienne, and opened it to a place held by a rectangle of white paper, between pages 78 and 79. On the recto the sentence was circled, in ballpoint,[90] "There's

---

[88] Daniel Dennett, mocking the Cartesian universe, has pictured, "a vision of the self as a sort of immaterial ghost that owns and controls a body the way you own and control your car" (*Consciousness Explained* [Boston: Little Brown, 1991]). My thesis departs from this point, reverses itself, and then comes back. As D. T. Suzuki used to say, "No difference, only the feet are a little bit off the ground" (quoted in Cage, *Silence*, p. 88).

[89] *Meaning and the Visual Arts* (New York: Doubleday, 1955), p. 23.

[90] I never write in books, and if I did I wouldn't use ballpoint, and if I did that I wouldn't circle passages; I'd underline.

Number of Items: 2

Barcode:0000280914292
Title:Death on the Riviera
Due:3/13/2017

Barcode:0000290156421
Title:Instant karma
Due:3/13/2017

Your material(s) are due on
the date(s) listed above.

---

. . .

2/20/2017          4:32 PM

nothing an actor enjoys more than a good juicy death scene."
There on the scrap, written in my own hand, were lines I
had taken from the endnotes to Edgar Wind's *Art and
Anarchy*[91] when reading it some 18 months ago:

Alfred Jary [sic], *Les monstres* (1895): "It is common usage
to call 'monster' an unfamiliar concord of dissonant elements. . . . I call 'monster' all original inexhaustible beauty."

Rimbaud, "Lettre du voyant" (1871): "It is a question of
making one's soul monstrous."

My first thought was Eve. She was on my mind because
I'd been seeking knowledge of her in the autobiography of
a woman with a similar name. This theory of reincarnation
does not make me very proud, but it holds more water
than the buy-one-get-one-free version that New Age types
employ to convince themselves that they are Caesar,
Voltaire, or Pocahontas. I have come to believe that each
new body is issued fragments of souls past. "On flows
the current," concurs Henri Bergson, "running through
human generations, subdividing itself into individuals."[92]

[91] (Evanston: Northwestern University Press, 1985) Too much art
and not enough anarchy in this book, but at least Wind is
churlish enough to violate *The Chicago Manual of Style*: "It is
desirable that the note section not overbalance the text" (15.44).

[92] Henri Bergson, *Creative Evolution* (New York: Modern Library,
1944), p. 294. Cf. Ron Rosenbaum, "What Does John Diebold
Actually Do?" In his *Manhattan Passions* (New York: Beech Tree,
1987), p. 134: "Do you know how they select the top lamas in
Tibet? When the old one dies, they go out into the countryside
and try to find a child who was born at the *exact instant* the lama
passed on. That way there is some assurance that the soul of the
lama leaped from the moribund body to be reincarnated in the
new baby."

There is some reason in Eve owning a piece of Eva, the actress who survived an explosion in the basement of her home[93] and whose father Richard Le Gallienne authored the inspirational *Anarchy in the Library*.[94] Eva Le Gallienne, born in 1899, did not die until 1989, but she wrote her autobiography in 1953, which, if that fact alone doesn't guarantee the soul's slow disintegration, ends with the assurance, "I have loved every moment of my life and I thank God for it."[95] Splat.

What year was Eve born? What happened to Eva that year? In all likelihood the 1968 heart attack represented a chunk of soul breaking loose from the actress and flying through the ether into the warm body of an infant girl librarian.

About this there can be no doubt: I had never seen or held the book before today. I could never forget the heft,

---

[93] She had gone down to the basement to help a servant light the stove when she struck a match without realizing the gas had been left on. "Had I opened my mouth and drawn a breath to scream, my lungs would have been fatally injured," she writes (p. 4). Her face and hands were badly scarred.

[94] (Chicago: The Black Cat Press), 1935. The work is what Le Gallienne called a prose fancy. The narrator is organizing his personal library when some of the books begin rioting for a more equitable system of organization, while some others fight to maintain the status quo. One little book calls out, "'Strike now, and the book unborn shall bless you.'. . . At this point a great folio that had been leaning threateningly, like a slab at Stonehenge, above the speaker, suddenly fell and silenced him" (pp. 11-12). "Sex was naturally the most unruly element of all [Amen!]. Volumes that had waited edition after edition for each other, yearning across the shelves, felt their time had come at last, and leapt into each other's arms" (p. 18).

[95] *With a Quiet Heart*, p. 302.

the scent of a book, the texture of the pages, or the typographic experience of the text once I have known it. This last sensation, described with simplicity in the colophon, or "note on the text," at the end of most good books, stays with me far longer than the words or ideas that the author has set down.

In photographs of her performances, Eva seems very comfortable with herself on the stage without feeling it acceptable to act naturally. The lady knew the advantages of looking beautiful. An actor who wants to do any more than that is treading on thin ice. As Hedda Gabler (1933), she sits back on an exquisite divan as if it is a bed of nails. As Mrs. Alving in Ibsen's *Ghosts* (1948), she sits erect listening for a whisper, more with her eyes than with her ears. The role must have suited her, since Emma Goldman, the lesbian anarchist speechmaker, saw in it the spirit of revolt.[96]

I concluded that neither Eve nor anybody else could or would have planted this list in anticipation that I would come across it. There are too many books in the library that I would have been just as likely to pick up. The list itself has no more meaning as a message of personal acknowledgment than it does as a document of my peregrinations in the library.

The urge to find meaning in coincidence is strong in me.

---

[96] "Those who like Mrs. Alving have paid with blood and tears for their spiritual awakening, repudiate marriage as an imposition, a shallow empty mockery" (E. L. Doctorow, *Ragtime* [New York: Random House, 1975], p. 45).

## Thursday 5 January

"I have examined myself carefully. I could never bid chaos welcome, throw bombs, blow up bridges, and do away with ideas. I am not an anarchist," confessed Hugo Ball,[97] not appreciating the timeless dilemma of the artist who is not an anarchist, which Madison Avenue knows, which Jesus and Shakespeare understood, which is that bombs do not do away with ideas; only ideas can do away with ideas. Though sometimes a bomb *and* an idea are needed.

## Friday 6 January

The Gatha of the Bell states, "The bell-sound travels in three thousand worlds / Buddhadharma spreads through myriad nations."[98] This program for world domination has survived many centuries because of Buddhism's practically viral method of contagion.[99] Randomness and chaos have spread from the ashram to the laboratory and the boardroom. The phenomenon of entropy is described in ecstatically Buddhist language: "All space will be at the same temperature. No energy can be used because all of it will be uniformly distributed through the cosmos."[100] And while the businessman once strove to subdue the anar-

---

[97] *Flight out of Time*, p. 19.

[98] Translated by Dorise H. C. Yang.

[99] Karl Jasper observes that "foreign religious forms become garments for Buddhist thinking and soon become Buddhist thinking itself" (*Socrates, Buddha, Confucius, Jesus*, p. 38). Speaking dialectically, you've got viruses, Buddhism, and entropy on one side, and DNA, dadaism, and fire on the other. In another sense, all six are equals.

[100] Lincoln Barnett, *The Universe and Dr. Einstein* (1948).

chist, he now embraces him.[101] The pyramid model of business leadership has given way to the shambles of the network, and the towering CEO has been replaced by an agency of phantom consultants.

### Saturday 7 January

"The most horrendous recipe"[102] for cacodyal (usually spelled without the second *a*) in *The Anarchist Cookbook* holds special appeal for me. Not only does it burst into flame the instant it is exposed to air, but I like that the dadaists were aware of this excitable, malodorous potion. A painting hangs in the Pompidou entitled *L'oeil Cacodylate* that is decorated with messages and signatures by such luminaries as Francis Picabia, Marcel Duchamp, and Tristan Tzara.

"Military TNT comes in containers which resemble dry cell batteries, and is usually ignited by an electrical charge."[103] An ordinary curling iron can act as a detonator. The bomber grips the handle, spreading the metal elements and tensing the spring. By choice, he can—or if disturbed or killed, he will—release his grip and the elements will make contact, completing the circuit and triggering the explosion. The experts call this mechanism a deadman switch.

---

[101] Tom Peters—a best-selling business writer invariably given the epithet "guru"—extols "chaos per se as the source of market advantage" (*Thriving on Chaos* [New York: HarperPerennial, 1994], p. iv).

[102] Powell, pp. 150-51.

[103] Powell, p. 118.

### Sunday 8 January

Fire burns *down* smaller cities, but Chicago has gone *up* in flames.[104] Young professionals, starving artists, and schoolkids kick up a fine dust that smells of burnt chocolate, fresh bread, and hot tar. Beneath the streets and in the air around the skyscrapers, the city continues to smolder a hundred years after the 1871 holocaust. Corner mailboxes still feel warm to the touch.

Chicago has nothing to compare to Broadway or Hollywood, with their flashpans and carefully controlled pyrotechnics. Actors know to avoid this city. When embarking on national tours, Rex Harrison and Noël Coward stipulated in their contracts that they would skip Chicago entirely, lest they fall victim to the vicious reviews of Claudia Cassidy, the *Chicago Tribune* critic. Our fires inflict lasting burns.

### Monday 9 January

Enormous bookstores are popping up all over the city. Today I entered one, not to purchase anything of course, but to look at *The Tibetan Book of Living and Dying*, AWOL from the library since at least June. I do not feel guilty about using the bookstore like a library. After all, they design them to look that way. The large bookstore of today is the hyperreal library of yesterday. Here are the books, but where is

---

[104] "Chicago specialized in the production, handling, and storage of combustible goods," recalls one historian of the Great Chicago Fire (Cromie, p. 11). Jack London called the city "the industrial inferno of the nineteenth century" (*The Iron Heel* (New York: Sagamore, 1957), p. 204n.

the dust? The chains have done away with the faulty light fixtures, the disorder of volumes that proves their usefulness, the surly-shy employees, and the uncomfortable promise of collective ownership and replaced them with decaffeinated cappuccino, bestseller discounts, and the spurious jingle of self-improvement through literacy. Lenin said that Fascism is Capitalism in decay. By trucking in millions of titles that ostensibly are for sale but that might as well be printed in Aramaic, these stores accelerate the decay by turning bookbuying into a practice of unfathomable complexity, inducing in men and women a momentary amnesia as they walk into the stores and gape at all the perfect spines, thinking "Now what was I looking for again?"

Bookstores are stores disguised as libraries.

I have learned from libraries that where you put a book matters. Shelve Thurber beside Machiavelli and watch how both become their opposites. Edgar Allan Poe next to Emily Dickinson remains decoration, but next to Betty Crocker it transmutes into something ghoulish. The system for shelving books in libraries seems chaotic, but it mirrors the system of nature. The library's system developed over five centuries in the weary minds of a thousand archivists insane for their inventories and has been mastered by no single human. The system in the enormous bookstore, on the other hand, is based on a simple song with the melody of "Twinkle, Twinkle, Little Star" and the lyrics: A, B, C, D, E, F, G.

### Tuesday 10 January

Hugo Ball says, in his own diary, "People who keep a record of their experiences are resentful, vengeful people whose vanity has been wounded."[105] Guilty. Every day I succeed as a diarist I fail as a writer. I can record in excruciating detail a thousand moments at the counter with Eve and jot down every striking passage I come across in the books I read, but doing so will in no way join my lips to hers or prove to anyone that I have acquired a certain prowess as a scholar.

If I lack the vocabulary and vision to compose the words to accomplish these objectives, I must take an action that will do so or—no, *and*—die trying. My prose may lack the tensile strength of Henry James, but I certainly can explode my own self along with the 1.6 million volumes that the state makes available to keep vagrants like myself occupied. My death triggers the bomb: my own fist unclenching in surprise at the moment the bullets crash into my bone and sever my spinal cord. The deadman switch fits perfectly into the religion of the Tibetan monks, who know that "the spiritual climax is reached at the moment when life ends."[106]

The religion I was born with, on the other hand, has left me so ill-equipped to handle such an enterprise that I require at least two solid months of intense study. Of my religious training I recollect only endless ceremonial meals where ritual significance was attached to the blending of antagonistic flavors: bread and salt, bitter herb and sweet apple *charoses*, noodles and pineapple. You couldn't pick

---

[105] Ball, p. 45.

[106] Carl Jung, *Pysche and Symbol* (New York: Anchor, 1958), p. 300. As Roger Shattuck said of Alfred Jarry, "While he was dying he was at liberty" (*The Banquet Years* [New York: Vintage, 1968], p. 217).

one dish you liked and stick with it; that would be an insult to the cook, to the rest of the family, and to the scavenging Ukrainian ancestor who had originated these recipes; you had to sample everything on the table and praise its robust flavor. You had to sit at the table until everyone was sure they couldn't eat another bite and had been questioned repeatedly on the matter. This preoccupation comes at the expense of a much more urgent concern. Jews care all about eating but nothing about dying.[107] Before a meal they recite perhaps a dozen specialized blessings for every variety of edible; before death they recite the all-purpose couplet:

Shema yisrael adonai eloheinu adonai echad!
Hear, O Israel: the Lord is our God, the Lord is One!
Baruch shem kavod malchuto leolam va'ed!
Blessed is His glorious kingdom for ever and ever!

### Wednesday 11 January

Lost again today, on Ashland looking for the Haymarket Memorial, which I later found out is in Waldheim Cemetery, miles and miles away. I got confused because of Ogden Avenue, a diagonal street that hits both Ashland and Grand, a fact known to me but still lethal, as I took it the wrong way for too long.

Perhaps I can take my wretched sense of direction as

---

[107] As Ludwig Feuerbach confirmed, "Eating is the most solemn act of the Jewish religion" (*The Essence of Christianity*, 1841, translated by George Eliot, 1854 (New York: Harper Torchbook, 1957), p. 116. "There is probably no religion that is less concerned with death," writes Mark Kurlansky in the *Partisan Review* (Spring 1994).

confirmation of my artistic nature. Jean Genet describes Alberto Giacometti thus: "I had in front of me someone who was never wrong, but who was always lost."[108] Gide universalizes this matter, saying, "Most artists, scholars, etc., are coastwise sailors who imagine they are lost as soon as they get out of sight of land."[109]

### Thursday January 12

This year the Olympics in Norway were upstaged when a gang of terrorists kidnapped from the art museum a square of cardboard brushed with milk-based paint—Edward Munch's painting *The Scream*. It should come as no surprise that a video camera recorded the crime; the vernacular phrase, *captured on videotape*, turned out to be pure irony. Climbing out of the window, one man fell down from the ladder before escaping with the artwork. But these were more than bungling thieves. Like Snoopy, who walked with a soap bubble between his teeth but tripped over his own feet, these terrorists were "deft and clumsy at the same time." Their simple demand took everyone by surprise. Instead of asking for money or the release of political prisoners, they laid the foundation of an ingenious new form of art on the ruins of an old one. Instead of bodies, cash, or power, they wanted a pure exchange of information. The work of art in return for air time. They wanted Norwegian television to broadcast an antiabortion documentary.

But the Norwegians wouldn't budge. They didn't care

---

[108] *Alberto Giacometti* (Zurich: Ernst Scheidegger, 1962), p. 55.
[109] *Journal of "The Counterfeiters,"* first notebook, 1 August 1919.

about one painting, a century old and not even made by Van Gogh or Claude Monet. Let's see whether Chicago cares more about its Public Library. Let's see whether the network affiliates will broadcast *The Lord's Prayer*.

### Friday January 13

To secure borrowing privileges, I signed a contract with the library: "I accept responsibility for the safekeeping of library materials borrowed against my card. I agree . . . to pay any fines or other charges imposed for late return, loss, damage, or mutilation of library materials subject to the provisions of the Illinois Statute, Chapter 38, Article 16B, and the City of Chicago Municipal Code, Chapter 23."

Doesn't an anarchist keep his word?

(Only kidding.)

### Saturday 14 January

When I am all done and they discover that I was not a criminal but an artist, the art critics will have to turn in negative reviews, because if right I am a very real threat to the civilization that the critics live off. They will say that I lacked a sense of beauty or that my aesthetic theories crumble under scrutiny. They will accuse of me of being a sham Tinguely,[110] a self-hating dadaist.

As McLuhan wrote, intending to be figurative, "You

---

[110] If even one critic mentions my name in the same column as Jean Tinguely, I will have succeeded. They have written things about him that I would die to have written about me. No, I *will* die to have them written about me. "One might say that his goal is to terrorize us" (Huelsenbeck, p. 132).

Ubu et la négresse

L' « *Almanach du Père Ubu* » de 1901 ne porte pas d'indication d'éditeur ni d'imprimeur. Il contient 2 pages de réclame pour les ouvrages parus ou à paraître chez Ambroise Vollard, 6, rue Laffite, qui se chargea de sa publication.

might as well start screaming about a house that's burning down, 'This is not the act of a serious man!'"[111]

Or Arthur Avalon, also intending to be figurative, "Who is there so perverse as to commence the excavation of a well to extinguish a fire which has already caught his house?"[112]

### Sunday January 15

In 1962 Tinguely went out into the desert, like another Jesus Christ, but where Jesus Christ experienced great visions produced by the devil, Tinguely experienced only the bright lights and bared flesh of the Las Vegas night. Where the son of God was offered "all the kingdoms of the world, and the glory of them"[113] and refused, the artist negotiated a handsome fee for setting of a pile of TNT in the desert, an artistic project titled *Study for the End of the World*—a destructive force destroying nothing, an expensive and noisy joke, at once a mockery of the weapons that threatened to end the world and a celebration of the anonymous artists who first made explosions in the desert: heat and light their paint, the endless sands their canvas.

Tinguely set off a great pile of dynamite for a small audience, though he would have done it even if there was nobody there to see. I admire him above all other so-called artists because Tinguely understood that ideally a work of art would exist without either the artist or the audience. He ventured to make art autonomous, eventually getting

---

[111] *Hot & Cool* (New York: Signet, 1967), p. 278.

[112] *Principles of Tantra* II (Madras: Ganesh & Co., 1978), p. 258.

[113] Matthew 4:8.

to the point where all you had to do was step on a pedal, and the machinery would whir and the great mechanical arms would swing about and decorate the page chaotically, producing sheet after sheet of art created by nobody.

Twenty-five years before Tinguely was born, Alfred Jarry, an extremely prescient critic, wrote this review:

"Meanwhile, after there was no one left in the world, the Painting Machine, animated inside by a system of weightless springs . . . dashed itself against the pillars, swayed and veered in infinitely varied directions, and followed its own whim in blowing onto the walls' canvas the succession of primary colors ranged according to the tubes of its stomach."[114]

### Monday January 16

The first two times I ever visited the library took place on Sunday, the nicest day of the week for that, despite what the mayor says.[115] The building stood isolated by a man-made lake in an unfamiliar part of town. Since that was the only time I was inside that library, I remember only the steel shelves, the mismatched plastic chairs, and the rust stain on the wall where a drinking fountain had once been. I was six years old. My father, who never knew what to do with me and who never visited the library himself, held my hand and walked along the shelves,

---

[114] Jarry, *Doctor Faustroll,* p. 238.

[115] According to Eric Zorn, Richard M. Daley "once said he sees no need for libraries to be open on Sunday because it's a day of religion" (*Chicago Tribune* [December 1, 1994], Section 2, p. 1). Since New Year's Day 1995, the library has been open on Sundays.

searching for a book he thought I would like, not knowing that a children's collection existed elsewhere. His gait showed exasperation at all the dull titles and depressing spines, but I was impressed with the way he operated by instinctive and trivial criteria—much how I find books in the library, to this day. Though unaccustomed to Scandinavian literature, he took the play called *The Father* as an encouraging sign, and he sat me down and read it in a voice that I now know was much too loud for the setting, though it did fall to a hush when he read some of the Captain's lines: "Didn't being a father sometimes make you feel ridiculous? I know nothing more absurd than . . . hearing a father talk about 'my children.' He ought to say 'my wife's children'!" "A man doesn't have children, it's only women who get children. That's why the future is theirs and we die childless."[116]

When we got home and my mother heard about our trip, she upbraided him in a shrill tone that she saved for the correction of his most thoughtless behavior. Learning mattered more to child development than did nutrition or hygiene. She took me right back to the car, and we drove to the other public library, which was bigger and closer. There were long colorful sofas and a mural of scenes from *Alice's Adventures in Wonderland*, a book I still have never read, that mural having spoiled my appetite. My mother conferred with the librarian and left me alone on the floor with Sarkis Katchadourian's illustrations of FitzGerald's *Rubaiyat*, and returned with an armload: *Uncle Remus*,

---

[116] August Strindberg, *Three Plays* (New York: Penguin, 1958), pp. 51, 73.

Babar, Christina Rossetti's *Goblin Market*, and William Rose Benét's *The Flying King of Kurio*, which described airplanes in such a stately manner: "Mother always wears a bonnet and gloves, because she likes to dress up a little for the ride."[117] I was overtired from the earlier trip, and this abundance of literature confused me and caused me to sob gently until falling asleep there on the library floor.

When I awoke, the same books were in my room with me. I remember a dire feeling of shock and shame: because she was ashamed of my tears, my mother had stolen the books from the library, and I was in possession of the goods. I pushed them under the bed and splashed cold water on my face for courage before joining my parents at the dinner table. During the meal they talked about the lawn, and I couldn't look at either one of them, and I couldn't eat.

I never wanted to see a book again. I decided to become a pilot, an occupation that required no reading material. My mother found the books under my bed and, laughing, explained that, yes, taking them home was okay, as long as I took good care of them and returned them by the date on the stamp. I studied the card from the inside pocket, looking at the signatures of all the people who had handled the book before me, and I experienced a great sense

---

[117] (New York: George H. Doran, 1926), p. 54. Soon afterward, I took out Benét's *Reader's Encyclopedia* (New York: Crowell, 1948) and looked up my name, David. "He killed Goliath, the huge champion of the Philistines." Then I looked up Philistines and found a quote from Matthew Arnold's *Culture and Anarchy*: "The people who believe that our greatness and welfare are proved by our being very rich." If this fails, the operative question will be Emily Dickinson's: "Was it Goliath was too large / Or only I too small?"

of communion with them, a smart and well-behaved alliance of people who knew how to treat a book.

### Tuesday January 17

When it comes to pivotal actions, chronicles written beforehand contain more truthfulness than those written afterwards. The words are written down first, and the words dictate the plans, the execution, and the eyewitness accounts. "How do I know what I think until I see what I say?"[118] men of action ask, and contrary to popular belief, men of action are always men of words.

You've got to christen a ship before it can sail.

History has repeatedly taught that you can no more reconstruct an assassination or bombing from the remnants than you can make architectural drawings from a building's ruins.

"The tiny ink marks of which a symphony consists may have been made long ago, but when they are fulfilled in sound they become imminent and mighty."[119]

Actors are jealous of authors because authors create, organize, and manipulate all the ideas before the actors ever get there, leaving only secondary matters of tonality and interpretation. Whether Sir Lawrence Olivier or Mel Gibson plays Hamlet, it all follows the same script.[120]

---

[118] E. M. Forster, *Aspects of the Novel*.

[119] Paul Bowles, *Collected Stories* (Santa Barbara: Black Sparrow, 1979), p. 48.

[120] "This I hold for incontrovertible," writes William Godwin, "the Actor has no right to correct his Author, and to make Shakespeare say what Shakespeare never thought" (quoted in *The Philosophical Anarchism of William Godwin*, by John P. Clark [Princeton: Princeton University Press, 1977], p. 85).

You know what I hate more than theater?
Improvisation.

### Wednesday January 18

Improvisation in music has nothing to do with improvisation in the theater. The latter relies on bankrupt beliefs about art and humanity, fostering a Nietzschean heartbeat in the chest of anybody with a voice that carries and who happens to be able to read. Jazz improvisation adheres to predetermined rules and rituals and concentrates on style rather than personality.

Rock and roll is theater. Kurt Cobain killed himself, we understand why. But why did Albert Ayler do it? Not a clue.

### Thursday January 19

Today on my way into the library to return *Habitations of the Word,* by William Gass,[121] I stopped to look at a color photographic portrait of the late Mayor Harold Washington, as in the Harold Washington Library, a portrait signed "Herbert." I looked him over, a trusting man in an expensive suit, an African American who came from nothing and earned the respect of millions. An articulate and brave politician whose commitment to education made him the obvious choice for a public library's namesake. I felt outraged at the Art Institute student who painted him in women's underwear. I experienced Washington as the antithesis of David Edgar Felsenstein,

---

[121] "You never know when an ugly penny might be found stamped with a rare mint mark or distant date" (New York: Simon & Schuster, 1985), p. 87.

biblioclast and pyromaniac, and thought about writing his family to explain that I didn't intend any slight to Harold Washington by blowing up the Harold Washington Library.

"Move along."

I spun around to see the man who had barked the order. He was black, far blacker than the man in the portrait. I noticed that, first, his color. Deep guilt for slavery, the Ku Klux Klan, and a half-dozen assassinations meshed with a superficial guilt for the crime I had just been caught in the middle of committing, which was . . . which was what?

And then I noticed his uniform. And his nametag, S. Dowdell. The guard reached for his walkie-talkie, looking vengeful and not at all patient enough to explain to me what I had done. I tried to speak. I felt like crying. Silas.

Suddenly, he cracked a smile, and then laughed with abandon and made as if he wanted to give me a hug. "Come here. It's okay, I was just playing. You've got to understand I'm in the library all day long. You're not mad, are you?" His laughter was irritatingly good-natured. I wanted to remind him that we were in a library, but, obviously, he knew that. I kept quiet. "I apologize," he said. "I didn't mean to scare you. Whew did you jump! I apologize and I tell you what. You borrow any book you want today at no charge. There's a special upstairs on poetry. Two for one."

Nice guy. Too bad about his upcoming leave of absence, though.

Faust's tragic error precedes the ambition, pride, and lust that are credited for his undoing as the play goes on. In the very first scene he disputes the only real truth in all the New

Testament, "In the beginning was the word,"[122] and from that moment on he is only fulfilling that capital misunderstanding. So as not to duplicate Faust's mistake, I must not waste any more time before writing my ransom note.

Dear Eve,

I am considering taking the books hostage. You

## Friday January 20

Why leave a ransom note? A device to conform to the conventions of terrorism? I'm new at this art form, and not yet confident enough to abandon convention.

Dear Eve,

I am taking the books hostage. Even though 80 percent of terrorists who take hostages succeed,[123] this endeavor will take all of my cunning and stamina, so please do not impose extra obstacles in my path, since doing so may very well result in collateral damage. I am well armed and admittedly not entirely competent with the weaponry. Moreover, experts have diagnosed me "emotionally stunted."[124] In other words, do as I say and nobody gets hurt. Together we can keep the exchange all at the level of pure information. I will hand you a list of my demands in a sealed envelope, and you will hand it to library security, who will turn it over to the police. I know how these things work, and I am prepared to negotiate. Whoever is

---

[122] John 1:1.

[123] Caroline Moorehead, *Hostages to Fortune* (New York: Atheneum, 1980), p. x.

[124] Not me actually, but my type, the individual with the terrorist mentality. Anthony M. Burton, *Urban Terrorism* (London: Leo Cooper, 1975), p. 5.

in charge can contact me by messenger or by cellular phone or by electronic mail. I will join the mayor in the library lobby and listen to what he has to say.

### Saturday January 21

Today I took home Stephen Hawking's *A Brief History of Time* and read the whole book, that is, I turned every page, without understanding a thing. Before I learned to read, I used to sit in my father's chair with a children's book called *Are You My Mother?*, which I would recite from memory as I turned the pages. When I thought somebody was watching, I'd shout, "I'm reading, I'm reading." Nothing has changed since then, only now I'm shouting, "I'm comprehending, I'm comprehending."

I can no longer read with patience or with any critical faculty; in fact, I can no longer read a book from cover to cover.[125] I continue checking books out because I like the titles, and I continue racing home with them, fanning through the pages and waiting for wisdom to poke me in the eye. I read a book pacing the floor or eating a meal, seizing on any zippy quotation to transcribe into this note-

---

[125] Sir William Waller caricatures the desultory reader, "running from one book to the other, as birds skip from one bough to another, without design; it is no marvel if they get nothing but their labour for their pains, when they seek nothing but change and diversion" (*Divine Meditations*). Seneca ridicules "people who never set about acquiring an intimate acquaintanceship with any one great writer, but skip from one to another" (*Letters from a Stoic*, II, 3). Only Robert Burton confesses to this sin: "I have confusedly tumbled over diverse authors in our Libraries, with small profit, for want of art, order, memory, judgement." (*Anatomy of Melancholy* [New York: Tudor, 1927], p. 13).

book, somehow convinced that if I write it down, I not only understand it but I came up with it myself.

Arthur Avalon has described my type: "Young men puffed up with their western education, but destitute of real worth, aimless and extremely lazy, show particular eagerness to learn this newly discovered Yoga, which presents itself to them as a religion which may be followed without any labor, trouble, or cost to themselves."[126]

### Sunday January 22

Havelock Ellis warned, "The artist life is always a discipline."[127]

William Powell advises that his *Anarchist Cookbook* "is for anarchists, those who feel able to discipline themselves on all subjects (from drugs, to weapons, to explosives) that are currently illegal and suppressed in this country."[128] How paradoxical, that anarchists need discipline.

Nor can the Buddhist let his mind drift.[129] I must stop treating the library like a whorehouse and every book in it like a fortune cookie.[130]

---

[126] Avalon, p. 235.

[127] Havelock Ellis, *The Dance of Life* (Boston: Houghton Mifflin, 1923): p. 277.

[128] Powell, p. 29.

[129] "Meditative Concentration," say the Tibetans, "is the king who rules over the dominion of the mind. The bodhisattvas have exerted great waves of Enthusiastic Perseverance, eliminating all laziness." *Lines of Experience* (Dharmasata, India: Library of Tibetan Works and Archives, 1973), pp. 8-13.

[130] Not that I hold anything against fortune cookies. One night I learned from one, "He who waits to do a great deal of good at once will never do anything."

Buddhists believe in one of two paths to enlightenment: the sudden versus the gradual, Vajrayana versus
Mahayana. Those who practice the latter, in such places as
Burma and Thailand, expecting enlightenment to come all
at once, have a better chance of catching a bullet with their
teeth. Ironically, Vajrayana, the kind practiced in Japan
and Tibet, means "thunderbolt." Yet it demands effort and
repetition. Nirvana comes incrementally.

### Monday January 23

Collecting books demonstrates taste, refinement, and
profound xenophobia. Borrowing them demonstrates
respect, humility, and self-destruction. Collecting books
organizes the mind and keeps the memory straight.
Borrowing them invites mental chaos and leaves sentence
fragments detached and swirling. Collecting books fosters
capitalism, and borrowing books demands anarchy.
Collecting books permits the leisure necessary for thorough contemplation. Borrowing books causes the waking
nightmare of time running out.

### Tuesday January 24

I don't ordinarily bring this notebook to the library, but
today I did because I intended to copy the ransom note on
the back of a recent library bulletin so I could deliver it to
Eve. On the way up to the second floor I found a copy of Sir
William Barrett's *Death-Bed Visions* on the stairs and was
immediately distracted by the chapter on "Music Heard at
the Time of Death." I carried the book with me a short way
to an unfamiliar alcove and read it through until the ending,

not finding a shred of useful information among the pages of small print describing pseudoscientific research into that most crucial of occasions, when life becomes death. I intended to write a letter to Barrett refuting his conclusions case by case, particularly his contention that "the soul is an *immaterial* entity, not simply a function of the brain,"[131] but before doing so I made up my mind to reread *The Astonishing Hypothesis*, by lapsed geneticist Francis Crick, whose neurological research has gone unnoticed. Crick advocates a strictly scientific account of the soul as a phenomenon inextricable from the biological functions of the human brain. In its essentials it upholds the pataphysical speculation of Alfred Jarry: "The brain, during decomposition, continues to function, and . . . its dreams are our Paradise."[132]

I traveled from one end of the library to the other looking for the Crick book, owing to a "B" in the call number that I thought was an "R." I also paused in the current periodicals section, where I read a dialogue on ugliness in the current *Harper's*[133] and a news item in *Art*

---

[131] Barrett, *Death-Bed Visions* (Wellingborough: The Aquarian Press, 1986), p. 170.

[132] Quoted in Nigey Lennon, *Alfred Jarry: The Man with the Axe* (Los Angeles: Panjandrum Books, 1984), p. 85. Crick curiously omits any mention of death in his book on the soul, though it may be assumed that that's what he means when he talks about rapid eye movement: "In REM sleep the brain waves are very similar to those in an awake brain, hence its other name, paradoxical sleep, since the person is asleep but his brain appears to be awake. It is in this phase of sleep that most of our hallucinoid dreams occur" (Crick, *The Astonishing Hypothesis* [New York: Scribner's, 1994], p.111).

[133] Between the publisher Françoise Giroud and the playwright Henri Lévy. Giroud: "Have you ever made love to a monster?" Lévy: "My case is of no interest" (January 1995: p. 25).

*in America* about a Finnish artist's plans for a work made of 10,000 trees planted "in a spiraling design derived from a combination of the golden section and the pineapple pattern."[134] When I returned I discovered that the notebook was missing.

Panic rolled down from every shelf. I retraced my steps as best I could, but I lost my bearings and seemed to cover the same areas of the library over and over, each time mistaking a Butterfinger candy wrapper wedged behind a cushion in a couch in the audio center, where I had been listening to Albert Ayler's *Witches and Devils*, for the gold cover of the notebook. I approached Eve's counter to ask her if anybody had turned the notebook in but veered away, knowing that my speaking voice would be frenzied. I convinced myself that I had left the notebook at home after all, but first I checked as many wastebaskets as I could find and all of the men's rooms. Flustered, but resigned to having to start all over again from the beginning, I made to go, only to find the notebook on the stairs leading to the main lobby, which came as a relief but brought on a brand new strain of anxiety. The familiar feeling of heartbeat steadying, breath deepening, an awareness of the metallic odor rising from my body, an urgent thirst.

Leaning against the banister, I flipped through the pages and read with new eyes the words I had written. I imagined I was somebody else, somebody stumbling across it and opening it with the perfectly honorable purpose of seeking some clue as to its owner and instead finding the convo-

---

[134] January 1995: p. 29.

luted theories and flippant digressions of somebody with unmistakable pretensions of a literary nature.

"Do anarchists vote?" "Will I write my way to reason?" "Why is *disorder* a synonym for *disease*?" "Doesn't an anarchist keep his word?" "What year was Eve born?" More than merely rhetorical, these questions assume a respondent, a readership that has contaminated this diary from the outset.

The experience of losing the notebook caused it to undergo a paradigm shift.[135] It went from being a diary to being a book, and as such it became just another combustible. "At such rare times you can feel the electrically charged neurons of the prefrontal brain realigning themselves like iron filings drawn by a magnet."[136]

### Wednesday January 25

Mrs. Bryars owns a copy of *Zen in the Art of Archery*, a manual full of useful advice for somebody who plans on walking into the library while squeezing the handle of a curling iron wired to a bundle of TNT: "It must be as if the bowstring suddenly cut through the thumb that held it. You mustn't open the right hand on purpose." Ideally, the hand will "burst open like the skin of a ripe fruit."[137]

The old girl has business out of town and has asked me

---

[135] "Often a new paradigm emerges, at least in embryo, before a crisis has developed far or been explicitly recognized" Thomas S. Kuhn, *The Structure of Scientific Revolutions.* Vol II, No. 2 of the *International Encyclopedia of Unified Science* (Chicago, University of Chicago Press, 1970).

[136] Joyce Carol Oates, "Zombie." *The New Yorker* (24 October 1994): 87.

[137] Herrigel, *Zen in the Art of Archery* (New York: Pantheon, 1953): pp. 48, 50.

to bring in her mail and water her house plants. She promised to cook me dinner when she gets back. Standing in my doorway, she described what she does with plain catsup and Cornish hens in such ecstatic terms that I felt myself about to take her into my arms. I should have invited her in; she looked like she had news, perhaps a reconciliation with Mr. Bryars, though I can't see how she'd have me over if he was going to be there. He couldn't have died, because the phone in her apartment continues to ring for hours every night.

She finally gave in and lifted the receiver, and the shock left him unable to speak, but, ever the optimist, she concluded from his silence that he wanted to see her. Now, as she's preparing for her journey, he's calling to say, no, wait there, don't come, don't come. She's combing her hairpiece, mending her hose, humming "Evergreen," oblivious to the ringing phone, and he's sitting half-naked in a motel room atop a bed done with hospital corners, the phone resting on one shoulder so both hands are free. Obsessed with his unsteady cardiovascular system, he wraps and rewraps the sleeve of the sphygmomanometer around his left biceps, eating nitroglycerin and breathing into a paper bag. The bathroom has been flooded since he tried to flush the motel Bible.[138] The room smells more like an infirmary than a hotel—rubber gloves, dead cells, and isopropyl alcohol. Walk through that door, and I swear to God there'll be a cardiac arrest here.

---

[138] Antipathy for scripture shows fear of death and denial of reincarnation. The fourteenth Dalai Lama wrote, "If belief in afterlife is accepted, religious practice becomes a necessity" (*My Land and My People* [New York: McGraw Hill, 1962], p. 50).

### Thursday January 26

Mrs. Bryars keeps shoes in the freezer, but so what? I keep library books in there. Nothing lasts, so you do what you can to retard spoilage.

### Friday January 27

I have this to say about all-pro capitalist O. J. Simpson: All anarchists are murderers, but all murderers are not anarchists.

I was born in Chicago in 1968, the year of the democratic convention, the last time that anarchy made a significant appearance here, but the chaotic plan of the streets has always reflected citizen-daydreams of freedom's logical extreme.[139] Meteorologists have documented a phenomenon they call the "lake effect," which dumps snow unexpectedly on the downtown area. Any metal you touch will give you a shock. Cold fronts sweep down from the Northwest, making the skyscrapers sway and disordering continuous thought.

This is the story of how the city went from trading post to "hotbed of anarchy."[140] It burned down in 1871, and the fire attracted anarchists like moths. They schemed and agitated; they squabbled with the socialists and gave clandestine lectures. They passed out leaflets and conned a few millionaires. In 1886, the anarchists rioted in Haymarket

---

[139] The musicologist Gunther Schuller wrote, in the liner notes to Ornette Coleman's *Ornette* (Atlantic SD1378, 1961), "One man's 'anarchy' is another man's 'freedom.'"

[140] Alexander K. McClure and Charles Morris, *The Authentic Life of William McKinley* (W. E. Scull, 1901).

Square, and in the confusion a rudimentary bomb went off, killing an officer of the law. Rather than scaring away potential radicals, the execution of the eight Haymarket anarchists became known as "the real beginning of the anarchist propaganda in America."[141] Their numbers grew, and their plans stretched beyond the city limits out into the world. They sent coded messages across the ocean. In 1894, an Italian anarchist named Cesario Santo killed France's President Carnot. In 1897, an anarchist assassinated Cánovas del Castillo, the prime minister of Spain and author of their constitution. Empress Elizabeth of Austria-Hungary, said to be beautiful and charming in *Webster's New Biographical Dictionary*, died the following year in like manner. Umberto I, king of Italy imposed martial law in 1898, and an anarchist got him in 1900.

The very same year, Leon Czologosz paid a visit to the Pan American Exposition in Buffalo, New York, found President William McKinley in its Temple of Music and shot him down. Czologosz was captured and sentenced to death, and federal officers traveled to Chicago to arrest the anarchists, including Emma Goldman, who had planted the ideas in his head. "She set me on fire,"[142] Czologosz had said.

### Saturday 28 January

In the library today there were signs of the arrangements they are making for the visit from the Tibetan

---

[141] Ross Winn, quoted in Paul Havrich, *The Haymarket Tragedy* (Princeton: Princeton University Press, 1984), p. 377.

[142] McClure and Morris, p. 440.

monks. In the main vestibule,[143] they hung a banner saying *Welcome* in a dozen languages. With velvet ropes, they cordoned off an area on the basement floor, directly below the first-floor oculus, where the monks are to create their mandala of sand. A pure white scrim has been unrolled over the floor. For a few days the mandala of the Tibetan monks will overlay the brass and terrazo work by Houston Conwill, *Du Sable's Journey*.[144]

They created a display with books of the Dalai Lama and other volumes, including *The Tibetan Book of Living and Dying*, which I have been searching for for the past three months. One of the library staff, maybe Eve herself, must have been keeping it behind the counter without checking it out. This theft certainly violates the librarian's code, but I am not sure whether to commend her or report her. I imagined Eve at home curled up with the book, sixty candles forming her halo. I pictured her in wool pajamas, the top open at the throat. I pictured thick wool socks slightly worn at the heel and the big toe. I stood before the book, longing to touch a book that Eve had read.[145]

---

[143] "Between the clitoris and the entrance of the vagina is a triangular smooth surface. . . . this is the *vestibule*" (*Gray's Anatomy*, p. 1027).

[144] Itself something of a mandala—with its four circles within a circle: (1) Acts of Hope, GRACE, and the Atlantic Ocean; (2) Acts of Temperance, SPEECH, and the Mississippi River; (3) Acts of Wisdom, VISION, and the Gulf of Mexico; and (4) Acts of Justice, BALANCE, and the Illinois River.

[145] "A restless spirit haunts over every book" (Jonathan Swift, *The Battle of the Books* [London: Chatto and Windus, 1908], p. 7).

In Mrs. Bryars's apartment I heard the ringing again and walked the floor like a crazy pup until realizing that it wasn't her phone after all. The ringing seemed to emanate from a place below her floor but above my ceiling. I experimented some, by standing in different places and letting myself slip into a relaxed state to better hear this elusive noise. Listening is simpler up here because Mrs. Bryars has wall-to-wall carpeting.

The condition I suffer from is named classical objective tinnitus, and the sounds are otoacoustic emissions. Not: there is a ringing in my ears, but: my ears are ringing. The human ear makes sounds, just as the fingertip has texture and the eye, color. "It is quite common," say the experts, "for normal ears to emit acoustic energy."[146] The human body constantly emits two noises, a high one generated by the nervous system and a low one generated by the circulatory system.[147] Mine just happens to emit a third, this dry, steady click-click-click-pause-click-click-click that origi-

---

[146] Dennis McFadden, *Tinnitus* (Washington, D.C.: National Academy Press, 1982), p. 18. My condition should not be confused with that suffered by John Self in Martin Amis's *Money: A Suicide Note*, who complains, "Owing to this fresh disease I have called tinnitus, my ears have started hearing things recently, things that aren't strictly auditory" (New York: Viking, 1985), p. 7. Leslie Sheppard and Audrey Hawkridge, in their *Tinnitus,* advise sufferers to "remember that tinnitus itself will not cause you to go completely deaf, nor will it cause your death, or cause you to lose your reason" (Bath: Ashgrove Press, 1987), p. 118.

[147] "A Sound accomplishes nothing; without it life would not last an instant" (Cage, p. 14).

nates in either the stapes, the eighth nerve,[148] or the cochlea.

Now that I know what the sound is, it no longer sounds like a telephone at all. I was lonely and I wanted to hear a telephone ringing, somebody who just called to say she loves me. "He that hears bells, will make them sound what he list," said Robert Burton.[149] Leonardo da Vinci knew of "the sound of bells in whose clanging you may discover every name and word you can imagine."

### Monday January 30

"I suppose this is why I keep a diary. . . . Fear of being forgotten is so compulsive I'd like to be remembered for each time I go to the bathroom."

—Ned Rorem[150]

"I hate quotation marks."

—David Edgar Felsenstein

(I hate the appearance of these bulky black sperm that, instead of penetrating the ovum of another person's words, seal them off from the rest of the text. I hate quotation marks for the simple reason that they remind me of all that I have not said.)

### Tuesday January 31

The telephone rang as I was napping on Mrs. Bryars's couch. The ring was unmistakable, and I answered.

---

[148] "The overwhelming majority of these tumors are not malignant." Ibid., p. 12.

[149] Burton, *The Anatomy of Melancholy*, p. 365.

[150] Rorem, p. 90.

"Mrs. Bryars?"

"No."

"Hello, Mr. Bryars, this is Jeanie from the Zion Lutheran Church. You may remember that our fine American flag was destroyed by arson last November. That flag meant a lot to the church and to the community, but the cost of replacing it is prohibitive. In order to make a flag that big, out of one cloth, not several pieces stitched together, you need an enormous loom. There are only two looms of that size operating in the entire country, and Ted Turner controls the one that makes the flags."

"I'm sorry."

"We're asking the community to contribute to the effort to buy a new flag."

"I'm so sorry."

"I understand. Thank you for your time, Mr. Bryars."

"I'm sorry, Jeanie."

### Wednesday February 1

This year the library is undertaking a major project to arrest the natural and artificial deterioration of its holdings. The staff has removed thousands of books and loaded them on trucks, which haul the books across the state line to workshops where trained personnel reglue and resew bindings, mend pages, and set them on conveyor belts to pass through fumigation chambers, a process oxymoronically known as loving restoration.

Look, I love books more than anybody does. I read them, I reread them, I copy passages from them into my notebook. A biblio-abolitionist, I respect books enough to refuse ownership of them. When Samuel Beckett died, there was nothing in his small Paris room but a single copy of Dante in the original Italian; I will go him one better. I have just over a month to get rid of the *Webster's New Collegiate Dictionary*, *The Holy Bible*, *Gray's Anatomy*, *The Anarchist Cookbook*, and the recently purchased *Tibetan Book of Living and Dying*, and then I'll die without a single book. I'll donate them to the library the day before. I love books but can't stand the thought of preserving them. If you accept the proposition that books are living things and "that books breathe,"[151] then this practice must be regarded as an unnatural prolongation of life, a desperate attachment to something fleeting and momentary, a futile exercise in cryonics.

"One master compares cryonics to going directly to a cold hell."[152]

My research has led me to the conclusion that anarchism and Tibetan Buddhism express essentially the same truths. They eschew sentiment and the fear of death for art and the acceptance of death. Things deteriorate and return to dust; the energy they once contained flows back into the universe. This process, known as entropy, gives us reason to rejoice. As Alma Jo Williams wrote in a letter to Harlan Ellison, "If you are for chaos, you are *pro-entropy*.

---

[151] Eugene Field, *The Love Affairs of a Bibliomaniac*. (New York: Charles Scribner's Sons, 1896), p. 164. Luciano Canfora has written, "The history of libraries of antiquity often ends in flames. . . . It is as if a greater force were intervening to destroy an organism that could no longer be controlled or checked" (*The Vanished Library* [Berkeley: University of California Press, 1990], p. 191).

[152] Sogyal Rinpoche, *The Tibetan Book of Living and Dying* (San Francisco: Harper, 1992), p. 377.

(It takes energy just to maintain the status quo. As the Red Queen said to Alice, 'You have to run as hard as you can just to stay in one place')."[153]

The work of art, like books and people, eventually will vanish from the earth if allowed to follow the natural course of things. Many modern artists, including Jasper Johns and Rabo Karabekian, the protagonist of Kurt Vonnegut's *Bluebeard*,[154] have created works that are fading and unraveling and that won't even survive to the end of the century. Such an artistic method undoes the evils of collecting, ownership, and the blinding effect of familiarity. Furthermore, it brings out the ardent if tragic love resembling the love that married couples feel as they enter old age.

Leonardo da Vinci could not have been ignorant of the relatively permanent fresco technique. By 1498, he was already a veteran artist, not to mention the greatest scientist in the world, and yet he chose not to paint the *Last Supper* as a fresco. He employed a medium of his own concoction. "Already in 1517," writes Kenneth Clark, "it had begun to perish, either through the dampness of the wall or some other mischance."[155] What remains on the Milan wall today, the work of restorers and charlatans, is simply a crass and insane mockery of the artist's conception of a work that would fade from the world.

The Tibetan Buddhists sweep away their sand mandalas for a reason: "The devotee progresses toward a

---

[153] Quoted by Ellison in *Future Life* 26 (May 1991).

[154] Karabekian painted with the acrylic wall-paint Sateen Dura-Luxe, which failed to adhere to canvas.

[155] Kenneth Clark, *Leonardo Da Vinci* (London: Penguin, 1989), p. 146.

higher level of awareness in which he is no longer dependent on the sculptural or pictorial image."[156] Leonardo, more dadaist-Buddhist than Renaissance man, gave his countrymen the perfect opportunity to achieve nirvana, and they squandered it.

### Thursday 2 February

Mrs. Bryars knocked on my door as I was counting the change from Dad ($591.49). I threw a towel over the booty and let her in. Her face was bruised and heavily made up.

"Everything okay up there?"

"The apartment looks great, David, thank you."

"And how is its occupant?" I felt I should be a little bit flirtatious with her.

"I happily resolved a little medical situation I had. And I'm fine. A little puffy."

"You heal fast," I said. "I can tell that about you."

Listening to her as she stood in my doorway, talking about how she was happy to resolve her "medical situation," I couldn't stop following the taut line of her jaw as it disappeared behind her ear. I thrilled at the precision and expertise of the surgeon's craft. I am tempted to say art, a term that could only apply to this particular surgical field, if, as Oscar Wilde said, "all art is quite useless."[157] The

---

[156] Amy Heller, *The Sacred Heritage of Tibet* Summer-Fall 1982 exhibition catalog, Beinecke Rare Book and Manuscript Library, n.p.

[157] Wilde, *The Picture of Dorian Gray*, p. 18. I don't at all think I'm being too literal about Dorian Gray, the character, whose face is more a work of art than is his portrait.

doctor files away at the bone until its shape pleases him, and he snips healthy human flesh, stretches it, and resews it in order to create a more advantageous relationship with the bone. Not a reversal of time, as is often said of plastic surgery, but an improvement on human evolution.[158]

This time when Mrs. Bryars mentioned Cornish hens, I was less hungry for them. In part, after contemplating the dark meat of the woman's face, I felt the urge to enlist in a strict vegetarian program. More disturbing, I sensed in my narrow universe that I stood at the center of her decision to have the surgery. I suspected that it all fit into some elaborate plan to entrap her polite, serious, young down-

---

[158] As such, plastic surgery has attracted a disproportionate share of those of us belonging to the "group evolutionary strategy" of Judaism (Kevin MacDonald, *A People That Shall Dwell Alone* [Westport, Conn.: Praeger, 1994]). When Jonathan Preston Haynes murdered Martin Sullivan, a Wilmette plastic surgeon, last year for creating "fake Aryan beauty" (*Chicago Tribune* [30 April 1994, Sec. 1, p. 1]), he showed a profound if muddled grasp of the intellectual questions that have surrounded the Jewish people since the Enlightenment. He objected to what he perceived as Dr. Sullivan's techniques for smoothing Semitic facial features. The Enlightenment led to the Reform movement, a brave attempt to create a space where a Jew could be a Jew and still remain a citizen of Germany. "We consider ourselves no longer a nation," announced the Pittsburgh Platform (1885). But they did not bother to check their plans with the German citizenry, who, it turned out, ridiculed any Jew who sought "to become such a fine gentilman just like a goymenera and to geeve up all fizonomie of Jewishness" (Oskar Panizza, *The Operated Jew* [1893] [New York: Routledge, 1991], p. 55). Roy Cohn, the archetype of Jewish self-hate, used to undergo a facelift every two or three years, according to his biographer (Nicholas von Hoffman, *Citizen Cohn* [New York: Doubleday, 1988], p. 395).

stairs neighbor, and I wanted to tell her, no, ma'am, it would never work. I do not lead a responsible life. My habits would disturb you. A relationship at present would interfere with my training as a Buddhist.

Moreover, I am already in love with Eve Jablom, the librarian, and if it doesn't work out with her, I've made plans to take my own life in the course of blowing up the Harold Washington branch of the Chicago Public Library sometime during the next month or two. Also, you're old enough to be my mother.

### Friday 3 February

A study of World War II kamikaze fighters traces their motive to a belief in "the inherent value of the sincere, self-sacrificial act, a value which is entirely irrelevant to its practical effectiveness."[159] Asians have a much firmer grip on suicide than do Jews, who illogically uphold the mass suicide on Masada as a moral and military victory over the Roman Empire, and, by an ahistorical extension, over Christianity. Asians merge an attachment to the self with a concession that the self is a meaningless construct, whereas Jews pretend that the value of their selves will soar if they are given over all at once—they want to buy salvation wholesale.

The Buddhist monks in Vietnam attained nirvana through self-immolation. They sat calmly engulfed in flame, oblivious to physical sensation. Relying on gasoline, they fell short of the greatest trick of all, spontaneous combustion. Talk about instant karma.

---

[159] Ivan Morris, *The Nobility of Failure* (New York: Farrar Straus Giroux, 1975), p. 183.

What mixture of chemicals could I ingest that would make my body into a bomb?

## Saturday 4 February

"All art is quite useless," says Wilde. "The right art is purposeless, aimless," the Zen master concurs.[160]

## Sunday 5 February

Every age produces its own prophet of the apocalypse. Walter Benjamin and Marshall McLuhan fulfilled this duty during the century's latest two periods of crisis. Benjamin said that "the extravagances and crudities of art," come out of the need for "a changed technical standard." For example, he writes, "Dadaism attempted to create by pictorial—and literary—means the effects which the public today seeks in the film."[161] McLuhan said that "so-called 'modern' art is always one technology behind."[162] This is what I say: the artist can only see a technology for what it is after it has been outmoded by a new technology. Painting only reached fulfillment after the invention of photography. Photography could not achieve its potential until the invention of film, etc. Burning down the library utilizes two technologies: (1) fire, the invention of

---

[160] Herrigel, p. 51.

[161] Walter Benjamin, *Illuminations* (New York: Schocken, 1969), p. 237. If A. Alvarez is right that "Violence, shock, psychopathic humor and suicide, these are the rhythms of Dada" (*The Savage God* [New York: Random House, 1971], p. 231), then Dada also anticipated the music and life of Kurt Cobain, leader of the rock group Nirvana.

[162] Tom Wolfe, in *McLuhan: Hot and Cool*, p. 41.

Prometheus, now that it has been rendered obsolete by the microwave oven and the neutron bomb, which cook things more efficiently and with less mess; and (2) the printed word, the invention of Guttenberg, now that it has been rendered obsolete by the microchip, which can store thousands of pages in the space of a Roosevelt dime.[163]

### Monday 6 February

*The Tibetan Book of Living and Dying* fails to live up to its promise of distilling the ancient *Tibetan Book of the Dead*. It has turned out to be a pandering and cheapening New Age text. "When a person commits suicide," it whines, "the consciousness has no choice but to follow its negative karma." "To embody the transcendent is why we are here."[164] How could Eve have an interest in such pabulum? Perhaps she isn't the girl I dreamed her to be.

### Tuesday 7 February

What about the film compels me? Why *The Lord's Prayer?* Because it "continually opens us to the range of

---

[163] Some historians have argued that inventions come along as soon as they are needed, but the need for this technology has been in place for a hundred years, at least since Mallarmé mockingly predicted, "All earthly existence must ultimately be contained in a book" (*Selected Prose Poems, Essays, and Letters* [Baltimore: Johns Hopkins, 1956], p. 24) and Flaubert wrote his novel *Bouvard and Pecuchet*—the theme of which was articulated by Lionel Trilling in his Introduction: "The human material has become intractable" (New York: New Directions, 1954), p. xxii.

[164] Rinpoche, p. 376; p. 91. Sogyal Rinpoche appeared in Bernardo Bertolucci's 1993 travesty *Little Buddha*.

God's economy and salvation"?[165] What do I hope to gain from exposing America to a prayer it already knows? Should I have to spell it out? Shouldn't an artist keep his intentions to himself? But am I the artist? Or is the director, Theodore Sultan? Were his intentions the same as mine? In what significant way is the world different now from 1916, the year the film was made? Did Sultan make the film with religious intentions or subversive ones? Is the answer in the film? Was the irony of a European Jew holding a placard with the words "Deliver us from evil" intentional? Or was the initial artistic statement engulfed by the subsequent ironies? Will this first meaning reveal itself when the film is shown on 1 million television sets?

### Wednesday 8 February

The library isn't burning, it's shrinking. Every single book on my list is missing from the shelves. My research cannot proceed without *The Cosmological Eye* by Henry Miller, *The Burning Library*, by Edmund White, *The Bomb* by Frank Harris, and *The Autobiographies of the Haymarket Martyrs*, and the *Harper's* magazine from January 1994 containing Philip Weiss's article, "The Book Thief," about Stephen Blumberg, who stole more than 18,000 books from 327 libraries and museums in the United States and Canada.

The library does not permit its patrons access to its database to find the names of other patrons who have

---

[165] *Catechism of the Catholic Church* (Mahwah, New Jersey: Paulist Press, 1994), p. 685.

checked out a specific book. I can't fathom how remote the chances are of another individual coincidentally reading all the books I want, but isn't that more likely than five separate individuals converging on the library, each there to retrieve one item from my list? No, the assassin acted alone.

Somebody out there came up with a plan identical to mine, consulting the identical texts and coming to the identical conclusions, which goes to show the obviousness of its logic.[166] I don't hold my bibliographic doppelgänger in any particular esteem. Neither one of us counts as a visionary. The zeitgeist comprises more than economic, cultural, and scientific indicators, but it doesn't hide from anybody, and it doesn't cost anything. It can be checked out of the library like any other book.

### Friday 10 February

Has my life proceeded according to a logical order? Do events from my childhood shed light on my current occupation? Does anything have anything to do with the early memory of seeing my initials, DEF, for David Edgar Felsenstein, on a shelf of books in the fiction section of the library? Do I have an artistic nature? Can an artist be an artist, even a conceptual artist, without being able to sketch? Do my grandiose artistic plans come from the

---

[166] The car was invented simultaneously on different continents, and the greatest literary and artistic ideas come from several minds working on the same problems, in other words, movements. From the sonnet and linear perspective through cubism and bebop, the most important things come from loose organizations.

frustration of being unable to draw? Do I want to achieve immortality through my art?[167] Am I a Jew, Buddhist, or Judas? Am I afraid to die?[168]

### Sunday 12 February

Today I had to check out Martin Williams's *The Jazz Tradition* because there was a line in it that I knew was there from a previous reading but could not immediately locate. As I approached the counter, Eve was emptying pencil shavings into a wastebasket. When she saw me, she came padding over. I say *padding* because it was obvious from her muffled gait that she was not wearing her shoes, though the counter prevented me from seeing her stocking feet.

"Comfortable?" I asked.

"Jazz?" she said. She was finally commenting on a book I had. "I hate jazz."

"It's an impure art form," I acknowledged, not knowing what that meant.

"Deedle deedle dee, deedle deedle deedle dee." She handed me the book.

Whatever else this journal may appear to represent—the ramblings of an overeducated paranoiac, "the defeat and

---

[167] Or, as Woody Allen joked, do I want to achieve immortality by not dying?

[168] In the words of Jorge Luis Borges, "Once dead, there will not lack pious hands to hurl me over the banister; my sepulchre shall be the unfathomable air: my body will sink lengthily and will corrupt and dissolve in the wind engendered by the fall, which is infinite. I affirm that the Library is interminable" (*Ficciones* [New York: Grove, 1962], p. 80).

despair of an effete nihilist,"[169] the penetrating observations of his generation's critical mind—it does not represent an accurate transcription of my daily thoughts. In order to do that, most every daily entry would sound like the ones before and after it: Eve, Eve, Eve's hair the color of a Kahlua bottle, the imperfect row of teeth in Eve's lower jaw, Eve's long, slender hands, her long, slender feet. Eve's hands and feet, four objects to marvel at individually and collectively.

Yes, but fetishes are the enemy of true love.

### Monday 13 February

I really intend to deliver the ransom note to Eve tomorrow at the library, but it needs serious revision. Today I will buy a proper pen and several sheets of 100% cotton bond paper. I do not intend to procrastinate any further. "You think you are simply resting," admonishes Beckett, "the better to act when the time comes, or for no reason, and you soon find yourself powerless ever to do anything again."[170]

### Wednesday 15 February

In all contemporary writing, I have found not one who speaks so directly to me and to my whole enterprise as Michel Foucault, the famous French intellectual and AIDS casualty. He is my theoretician and I am his artist. Foucault situates the twentieth-century author not in the world but in the library. He exhorts me, by way of a bomb metaphor: "Modern literature is activated—Joyce, Roussel, Kafka,

---

[169] A characterization of the music of Miles Davis. (Williams, *The Jazz Tradition* [Oxford: Oxford University Press], 1983), p. 212.

[170] Beckett, *The Unnamable* (New York: Grove, 1958), p. 3.

Pound, Borges. The library is on fire."[171] Welcome to the culmination of modern literature. Burn, baby, burn.

## Thursday 16 February

Why am I going to all this trouble, anyhow? What do I expect to achieve by blowing up the library? Aren't my intentions basically selfless? Is anonymity desirable? Is there an historical precedent for what I am doing? Does the burning of the Library of Alexandria in 650 A.D. count? Am I disingenuous for finding justification for book-burning in a book? Didn't I once give the book-burners in Ray Bradbury's *Fahrenheit 451* credit for spurring Montag and the other renegades to read and memorize Plato, Confucius, Einstein, and Thomas Love Peacock? Do the Nazi book-burners also deserve thanks for the academic zeal of Jews?[172]

---

[171] *Language, Counter-Memory, Practice* (Cornell: Ithaca University Press, 1977), p. 92. I confess to initial bafflement at the inclusion of a composer in a field of writers, until I realized he was referring not to Albert-Charles-Paul-Marie but to the poet, Raymond Roussel, author of *Locus Solus* and subject of Foucault's study *Death and the Labyrinth*.

[172] Dear Kitty, it surprises me to have Nazis as allies. Never mind the guilt over betraying my heritage, I am dispirited by the unconvincing contour of my argument. Tom Phillips, writing about the art of collage, warns against "the perilous ease with which Auschwitz can be united with Buddha" (*Works and Texts* [New York: Thames and Hudson, 1992], p. 119). Like a collage, this journal takes meanings and rips them from their contexts. In my efforts to amass evidence and marshall support for my project, I am raping literature and violating authors and not convincing anybody, because I have gone about it all wrong. Every time I have had to decide whether to borrow another's phrase or to devise one of my own, I have taken the easy way.

### Friday February 17

"Explosives Sales and Consultation: Your Vengeance Is Mine." The one classified ad with a local phone number in the back of the *Guns & Ammo* that I bought in November. The voice on the other end of the line sounded like that of a hyperactive child. He claimed to be Nathaniel Stone, grandson of local billionaire W. Clement Stone,[173] and when I said I needed TNT, he said he didn't talk on the phone but he could be here in ten minutes.

Nathaniel pulled a blue canvas Samsonite suitcase up to my door. I reluctantly opened the door and invited him in. He wore dirty jeans and a black AC/DC T-shirt. He was my approximate age and height but thinner, and he grew his nails and combed his white-blond hair over his face. Refusing to take a seat, he crouched instead, like a sprinter, and looked down at the carpet when addressing me.

"Nice place. What do you pay?"

---

[173] Author of *Believe and Achieve* and *The Success System That Never Fails*

"Three fifty, not including heat. Can I get you some water?"

"Nice neighbors?"

"One lady upstairs makes me dinner every once in a while."

"But she doesn't cook as well as your mother, right?"

"To tell you the truth," I said, "I don't remember my mother ever cooking. The stove exploded once when I was a child, and after that we ordered out."

Nathaniel told me he wouldn't take a check, and I told him that was no problem, I had plenty of currency. He sold me two bundles of TNT for $175. He said a few things about how to attach the 12-volt dry cell, which he threw in at no extra charge, but when he saw the befuddlement on my face he agreed to rig the bomb himself, sending me out to get a quarter-inch curling iron and either a roll of wax paper or a pack of Necco Wafers.

The appearance at my door, in a third the time it takes for a pizza to be delivered, of this scoliotic, effeminate bomb technician, stirred me to recklessness, or why else would I have skipped into an Osco Drug and purchased candy and a dual-setting, lavender-handled curling iron without giving a thought to the curiosity it might raise? Not until I got out of the store did I remember that a twenty-six-year-old man with perhaps a half-inch of growth on his scalp would have no use for a curling iron other than rigging an explosive device.

Nathaniel did a little joyful dance upon my return, as if he'd thought I was going to abandon him in my own apartment. When he lifted his arms, his shirt came untucked and I could see his ribs and his hairless white stomach. He wore his pants high, like a girl, so I could not see his navel. At his feet was a packet encased in bubble wrap and electric tape, small enough to fit discreetly into a gym bag. He took the curling iron and the Neccos from me and crouched down to finish building the bomb. The exact shape and size of quarters, the chalky candy spilled to the floor.

More than Nathaniel's appearance unnerved me, his asking about my mother, for instance. I had said nothing specific about my plans, yet he acted almost as though we had discussed them at length, though, if he found my diary in the freezer while I was away, he showed no guilt. Maybe he had seen me in the library, though if I had ever seen him I would have remembered it. He fished out of his suitcase a library copy of Stéphane Mallarmé's *Selected Prose Poems, Essays, and Letters*, which contains "The Book: A Spiritual Instrument," and offered to lend it to me indefinitely. "They form a tomb in miniature for our souls," Nathaniel quoted, and, smiling at the floor, he told me of a book collector in ancient times who could not bear the thought of others reading his codices after his death, so he ordered the servants to use them as bricks for his funeral pyre. He said he read the story but didn't bother to note where. Unbelievable.

Nathaniel asked me if I had thought of cacodyl, saying that not only does it create a gorgeous fireball that would spread quickly in a building with so much paper, but it also gives off an overpowering garlicky stink—which he thought would be a nice touch. His slender hands moved quickly and his voice sounded high and strange. I never knew that we had such cunning and depraved creatures right here in Chicago.

## Saturday February 18

"How we spill that seasoned life of man preserved and stored up in Books; since we see a kind of homicide may be thus committed, sometimes a martyrdom, . . . a kind of massacre."

—John Milton, *Areopagitica*

## Sunday February 19

After all the hours I've logged there, I still lose my way in the library. Today I set down a copy of Flaubert's short story "Bibliomania"[174] when I remembered I had left the copy I had made of the front page of the *Chicago Reader*[175] at a copier on another floor. The feature, "Building Boom," surveys local architects about the building whose destruction they would most applaud. It includes photographs of the buildings they named, manipulated to look like they are being blown up. The front page depicts the destruction of the runaway favorite, the Harold Washington Library.[176]

---

[174] "He loved a book because it was a book; he loved its odor, its form, its title" ([Evanston: Northwestern University Press Library, 1929], p. 11). Cf. Aliki, *How a Book Is Made* (New York: Harper Trophy, 1986): "I like books. / I like the way a book feels. / I like the way a book smells."

[175] 5 August 1994.

[176] The results took me by surprise. Though architecturally deaf, I had read effusive notices of the library. Vincent Scully said it was "built of the very bones and blood of Chicago" (*AIA Guide to Chicago* [New York: Harcourt, Brace & Co., 1993], p. 60). "This library stands apart," wrote Witold Rybczynski. "It didn't make me feel like a consumer, or a spectator, or an onlooker—it made me feel like a citizen" (*Atlantic Monthly*, August 1992: p. 87).

First, I had trouble remembering which copier I had used. Mirthful at the thought of somebody coming across the image of an exploding library, I thought a superstitious type might consider it an omen generated by the copying machine gods. Once I found the copier and the copy, I could no longer remember on which floor I had been reading Flaubert, and I grew anxious at carrying a picture of an exploding library on my person. Having a newspaper photograph of an event before it happened felt wrong. The picture made me wonder why I should bother, when the document already existed. If I found somebody's obituary, plotting to murder them would be redundant.

I took the elevator to the top floor, the blue-gray Winter Garden, where I stared out the windows and imagined myself thrown by a blast of TNT, carried bloodied and unconscious out above the city then dropping toward the sidewalk on the other side of State Street. I caught myself dreaming that two angels, both of them with Eve's face, would catch me.[177] By then I had absolutely no clue where Flaubert was, so I simply left the building.

### Monday February 20

A merry but dirty gang of early teens gathered today in front of the library on Congress Parkway. They had rap music and skateboards but seemed vaguely confused as to what to do with them, since there are no steps. Nevertheless

---

[177] Norman Mailer has concluded that "men who are otherwise serious but ready for personal violence are almost always religious" (*Violence in the Streets*, edited by Shalom Endleman [Chicago: Quadrangle, 1968], p. 87).

they felt they had come to the right place, a monumental public edifice of granite and red brick. As I was coming out around midday, a woman in a hat walked by with a Lhasa apso,[178] and one of the kids, a girl with a boy's hairstyle and shoulders, slid in front of her and skidded to a halt, so that they were facing each other. Somebody stopped the tape, and, instead of silence, the sounds of the city reappeared. The girl on the skateboard asked, in, surprisingly, a French accent, "Can your dog bite me?"

When I got home, I saw men loading Mrs. Bryars's things into a truck. I don't know whether she died or just moved.

### Tuesday 21 February

What would my father say if he knew what I was doing? My mother? Would they regret taking me to the library when I was young? If they had known what was going to happen, would they have withheld books from me, kept me at a safe distance from learning and knowledge? Would they have refused to take me to view art in museums? Would they have prohibited television, movies, music, education? Would they wish they could exchange me for John Berger's "man brought up from birth in a white cell"? "He has never seen anything except the growth of his own body. [His] gestures might be passionate and frenzied but to us they could mean no more than the tragic spectacle of a deaf mute trying to talk."[179]

---

[178] A Tibetan breed of terrier; I can take anything and turn it into a sign.

[179] *New Statesman*, 22 November 1958.

## Wednesday 22 February

Destruction of the Harold Washington Public Library will mean the loss of 4.5 million U.S. and 2 million British patents; a Civil War collection including photos, letters, and 7,000 books; 800 first and rare editions by Chicago authors; more than 13,000 World War I and World War II posters; and 24,000 dance band arrangements from the thirties, forties, and fifties. All of these resources are now imprisoned in archives, while other, ostensibly more utilitarian sources are being scanned for CD-ROM and the World Wide Web. Burning the books will liberate them. As Rabbi Ben Joseph Akiba said, "The paper burns, but the words fly away." I am reminded of the American Library Association's World War I propaganda poster, which proclaims: "Knowledge Wins: Public Library Books Are Free."

## Thursday 23 February

It would not be an exaggeration to say that I am sleeping and eating half as much as when I first began giving myself magnetic treatments, and yet my strength and stamina are terrific. The blood used to roll dopily through my arteries, and now it courses with vigor. This morning I feel alert and steady, a result of having purged the toxins and gradually tuned specific geophysical elements in my system with those in the air.[180]

---

[180] "Consciousness arises from physical interactions between electrical and magnetic products of the brain and ambient electrical and magnetic products in the environment," according to Stephen M. Kosslyn, "Cognitive Neuroscience and the Human Self," in *So Human a Brain*, edited by Anne Harrington (Boston: Birkhäuser, 1992), p. 48.

Unfortunately, the condition that I meant to cure with these treatments has not subsided. I still constantly get lost indoors and out. The magnetic forces coming from within me[181] have overloaded my delicate sense of direction. Werner Heisenberg has described an individual such as I, "in the position of a captain whose ship has been built so strongly of steel and iron that the magnetic needle of its compass no longer responds to anything but the iron structures of the ship."[182]

### Friday 24 February

A week of record lows. Cold and grimy until springtime, Chicago kneels and prays for an event to take people's minds off the weather. Something to replace stories about homeless refusing to take shelter, old ladies frozen to basement floors, and frustrated dogs attacking their masters. The city needs a fire to melt the ice—a very specific kind of fire. Polonius warns his daughter of blazes "giving more light than heat";[183] such a fire as the one I am proposing has proved to generate heat. The books of the Library of Alexandria were fuel enough to heat four thousand public baths for six months.[184]

For a sick city, book burning also has therapeutic bene-

---

[181] A. S. Presman has said that "living tissues must be regarded as a weakly magnetic substance" (*Electromagnetic Fields and Life* [New York: Plenum, 1970], p. 4); but I have gone too far.

[182] *The Physicist's Conception of Nature* (London: Hutchinson, 1958), p. 30.

[183] *Hamlet,* by William Shakespeare (I.iii.117).

[184] Canfora, *The Vanished Library,* p. 99. Marc Drogin, in his *Biblioclasm* (Savage, MD: Rowman and Littlefield, 1989), speculates that between 500,000 and 700,000 volumes were burned in either 642 or 647 A.D.

fits nearly forgotten. In Plato, "the ashes of books, when mixed with ointments and potions, were . . . recommended for the curing of fistulas, tumor, calluses, constipation, dysentery, elephantiasis, hemorrhaging, eye inflammation, ulcers, and other ills."[185]

## Saturday 25 February

My parents deserve acknowledgment. They have supported me no matter what I did. When I quit school before completing my thesis,[186] my mother showed enough decency to keep her distance, mailing me a rhubarb pie she baked herself and a *Time* magazine feature on twentysomethings: "They have trouble making decisions. They would rather hike in the Himalayas than climb a corporate ladder. They have few heroes, no anthems, no style to call their own."[187] My father called in some favors

---

[185] Charles Isaac Elton and Mary Augusta Elton, *The Greek Book Collectors* (London: Kegan Paul, 1893), p. 95. Arthur Stanley Pease, in his "Notes on Book-Burning" (*Munera Studiosa for W. H. P. Hatch* [Cambridge: Cambridge University Press, 1946], p. 97), notes that "if a man fell ill who (like many in his time) considered the books of Epicurus to be poison, the only way to recovery. . .was if he, burning the books of Epicurus and kneading the ashes of the godless and impious and effeminizing letters with moist wax, and making an application of this, should bind about the stomach and all the chest with bandages."

[186] Having come across a remark in the margin of a letter from Piet Mondrian to James Johnson Sweeney in 1943, "I think that the destructive element is too much neglected in art," I sought to prove by arithmetic that the de Stijl artists directly caused the bombing of Hiroshima and Nagasaki. At least I managed to escape with a master's degree from the University of Chicago.

[187] David M. Gross and Sophfronia Scott, "Proceeding with Caution," *Time* (July 16, 1990).

# CALENDRIER
## DU PÈRE UBU
### POUR 1901

*Approuvé par Mgr St Bouffre*

| | | JANVIER | | | | FÉVRIER |
|---|---|---|---|---|---|---|
| 1 | M | DECERVELAGE | | 1 | V | Ste Tignasse |
| 2 | M | *St Macaire d'Alex.[1] | | 2 | S | St Schisme |
| 3 | J | *Ste Bertille, *vierge et Vve* | | 3 | D | *St Remezy, *évêque* |
| 4 | V | *Ste Oringue, *vierge* | | 4 | L | St Anal |
| 5 | S | St Birbe | | 5 | M | Ste Delpot, *mère* |
| 6 | D | *St Fursy, *abbé* | | 6 | M | *St Barzanuphe, *sold.* |
| 7 | L | *St Pelade, *évêque* | | 7 | J | Ste Gidouille |
| 8 | M | *Ste Goule ou Gudule | | 8 | V | COPULATION |
| 9 | M | *Ste Basilisse, *vierge* | | 9 | S | *St Apollon |
| 10 | J | St Bateau | | 10 | D | *Ste Zuarde |
| 11 | V | Ste Gale, *abbesse* | | 11 | L | *St Cémon, *chantre* |
| 12 | S | St Poil | | 12 | M | *St Vêle, *moine* |
| 13 | D | St Sagouin | | 13 | M | St Hérold, *évang.* |
| 14 | L | *St Hilaire | | 14 | J | St Ciput |
| 15 | M | St Terme | | 15 | V | Ste Crapule |
| 16 | M | Ste Girafe | | 16 | S | Ste Soupe |
| 17 | J | *St Antoine *abbé* | | 17 | D | AEROSTATION |
| 18 | V | *St Léobard, *reclus* | | 18 | L | *Ste Prépédigne, *mart.* |
| 19 | S | Ste Asperge | | 19 | M | *St Gabin, *prêtre* |
| 20 | D | St Grumeau | | 20 | M | Ste Marmelade |
| 21 | L | St Bol | | 21 | J | *St Pépin de Landen |
| 22 | M | St Dimenche, *abbé* | | 22 | V | *St Abile, *évêque* |
| 23 | M | *Ste Messaline | | 23 | S | SABBAT |
| 24 | J | *St Babylas | | 24 | D | CONCERT LAMOUREUX |
| 25 | V | REPOPULATION | | 25 | L | *Ste Valburge |
| 26 | S | *St Profit | | 26 | M | St Fouquier, *apôtre* |
| 27 | D | *St Avit, *martyre* | | 27 | M | *St Galmier, *sous-dia.* |
| 28 | L | St Etronge | | 28 | J | FIN DU MOIS |
| 29 | M | Ste Bardane | | 29 | | *Hunyadi.* Ste PURGE |
| 30 | M | Ste Bourboule | | | | |
| 31 | J | Ste Touche | | | | |

1. Sont précédés d'un astérisque les prénoms empruntés au livre officiel intitulé : *Prénoms pouvant être inscrits sur les registres de l'état civil destinés à constater les naissances conformément à la loi du 11 Germinal an XI.*

and secured a high-paying position with a downtown bank. When he heard that I'd showed up for the interview in my new Brooks Brothers suit and a paper bag over my head, he said he understood, he read the article, too. Though I sometimes resent him paying my monthly allowance in coins and small bills, he undoubtedly does it out of love for his only child.

I wouldn't be writing about my parents if I wasn't thinking about posterity, in fact I wouldn't be writing at all.[188] In the last hour a week has gone by. My own death is already past me, and now my mother and father have come across the words written in a yellow notebook singed but not destroyed by the blast. Each blames the other for not teaching me about respect for public property. Each thinks that the tiny script and illegible footnotes filling these pages look like the type of thing the other would like. They decide to say nothing to the reporters. Hi Mom! Hi Dad!

### Sunday February 26

In 1901, an English scientist named W. S. Small published the second part of his study on the mental processes of the rat, which introduced the maze method into the study of animal intelligence.[189] If ability to navigate an elaborate network of passageways determines an animal's intelligence, then I have to conclude that I am not too intelligent. There is no way I could have found my way

---

[188] Yet again. David Edgar Felsenstein, the "ever self-ending dadaist."

[189] Edwin G. Boring records the moment in his *History of Experimental Psychology* (New York: Meredith, 1929).

through the Hampton Court maze, a rat-size reproduction of which was used by Small. I would race headlong into a maze and backtrack, humbled but no wiser, straight into the Minotaur's lair. I feel so smart as I study my precious books and record what I consider to be original thoughts in this journal, but if I can't find my way home afterwards I must be dumber than most cats and dogs.

The difference between a maze and a labyrinth is that a labyrinth is circular, like a mandala. The monks are almost here; let's see if I can find my way out of their labyrinth.

### Monday 27 February

A burning library might strike a familiar note with the monks from Tibet. According to L. Austine Waddell, 30,000 *Bhikshus*, or Buddhist monks, came from "Alasadda," "considered to be Alexandria," the site of the most famous biblioclasm ever.[190] In modern times, Tibetans have survived the destruction of six thousand of their temples along with vast libraries and countless artistic treasures.[191] They have survived Chinese ruthlessness and global apathy. They should understand my

---

[190] *Tibetan Buddhism* (New York: Dover, 1972), p. 9. Waddell, one of the first Westerners ever to enter Tibet, gained knowledge of the religion by purchasing a temple. The priests, he says, "convinced themselves that [he] was a reflex of the Western Buddha, Amitabha, and thus they overcame their conscientious scruples, and imparted information freely" (p. ix).

[191] 1995 pamphlet published by the Tibetan Aid Project. Book-burning appears in Chinese history, too. Max Weber, in his *Religion of China*, chronicles a moment where "the enemy of the literati who instigated the burning of books was united with the literati" (Glencoe: The Free Press, 1951), p. 87.

project more readily than Chicagoans, since so much of my inspiration results from Tibetan texts. However, a mission of fundraising, rather than culture or religion, brings them to Chicago. After the bombing of the World Trade Center in 1993, the monks created a mandala for peace, and the donations rolled in like never before. In order to drum up more business, they left behind the Buddhist detachment and elegant anarchy that attracted me to them in the first place. Somehow I've got to communicate to them that I believe in their cause, and in no way intend to stir up any negative publicity for them.

### Tuesday 28 February

Including the long opening shot of the white building, before the rabbi comes out, the video by Theodore Sultan lasts eight minutes. The box says eleven. The three missing minutes must come from the ending, since the tape ends abruptly with the word Amen. I doubt the rabbi of *The Lord's Prayer* is a real rabbi. He averts his gaze from the camera with a humility absent from true clergy. Maybe Theodore Sultan, the artist and arsonist named in the catalog, plays the rabbi. I wish I knew more about him. If nothing else, I am a thorough researcher, and the dadaist movement is among the most well-documented of the century, yet he doesn't show up anyplace in the diaries, letters, or interviews. Maybe Sultan never existed and somebody in this decade made the video as a big hoax. If he is a fraud, I relate to him as a fraud. It takes a counterfeiter of great imaginative power to propel the pseudointellectual to commit an act of false bravery and sham terrorism.

# Please direct my donation to:

**General Assistance:**
*For specific relief projects, construction projects, and development funds.*

❏$35  ❏$55  ❏$100  ❏$1000  ❏$5000  ❏Other: $_____

**Traditional Art and Literature:**
*To pay shipping on books and religious art to Tibetans.*

❏$____ for printing  ❏$____ for shipping  ❏$____ for recycled paper.

**Basic Support for a Monk or Nun:**
*To help with food, clothing, housing and educational materials for study.*

❏$30 per month ongoing pledge  ❏ $365 one year pledge.
❏ One-time donation of $_____

**Bodh Gaya World Peace Ceremonies:**
*For pilgrimage to Buddhist sites.  (Western visitors are welcome!)*

❏ $150 for a monk/nun's ten day pilgrimage.
❏ $_____ for general support of the ceremonies.
❏ Please ask the assembly to say prayers for_____.
❏ Send information about participating in a pilgrimage to India and Nepal.

**You can help in more ways:**
*TAP also has income generating projects.  Please indicate projects you are interested in:*

❏ Jataka Tales for children  ❏ Tibetan Prayer Flags  ❏ Video rentals
❏ Books on Tibetan refugees and history  ❏ Tibetan cards and calendars

**❏ I would like to help TAP distribute brochures in my area.**

---
Name
---
Address
---
City          State     Zip     Country
---
Phones:  Home          Work          E-Mail Address

**The Tibetan Nyingma Relief Foundation is a non-profit, tax-exempt organization.**
**Donations are fully tax deductible.  Federal Tax I.D. # 23-7433901.**

Like a baseball team in saffron robes, nine Tibetan Buddhist monks piled out of a bus and entered the Harold Washington Library Center this morning. I watched them unpack their sand and tools for awhile, but, after observing a news crew show up only to be told there was nothing to shoot until Friday, I got bored and went up to the fifth floor to look up the state laws for terrorism and destruction of public property. When I went down to check on their progress, I spotted Eve having a conversation with one of the monks, a stocky one with fair skin and thick glasses. She was gesturing frenetically, trying to communicate something about food or eating—chopstick and a bowl. When he got it, he laughed and nodded, and then she laughed, too. I had never seen Eve laugh before; even she seemed surprised at the sound coming out of her.[192]

As I got down to the lobby, I saw Eve walking out with the monk, ignoring me. I pushed through the doors in time to see them driving away in a gold Lexus with the license plate 3 TIBET.

---

[192] James Hilton wonders, "This Lama business may be all right for an old fellow . . . but what's the attraction in it for a girl?" (*Lost Horizon* [New York: William Morrow, 1934], p. 135). But I wondered no such thing. Beneath their robes throb glandular monstrosities trained by years of Tantric study. Above all, theirs is a religion centered on sensual ecstasy, which they pretend has a spiritual component. In his *Occult Glossary*, Guy de Parucker confirms that "Tantrik worship in many cases is highly licentious and immoral."

A famous movie actor is underwriting the monks' visit to Chicago. For several years he and his supermodel wife have passionately espoused their cause. This morning he appeared in a saffron robe and posed for pictures with the monks. He urged reporters to step up their coverage of the crisis in Tibet. With some coaxing, he recited a memorable line from a gangster movie that made him famous. "Count backwards from one hundred." Everyone, including the "hostile, inscrutable monks,"[193] gave him a wild ovation, which he acknowledged by lifting the skirts of his robe to give a shaved, muscular curtsy.

The fair-skinned monk approached the actor and whispered something into his ear. The actor nodded and handed him some keys. The keys to the gold Lexus, I determined, and this time I raced out and hailed a cab, something I have not done in all my years in Chicago.

I instructed the driver to follow the Lexus, which took Congress to Michigan and turned left, passing the Art Institute of Chicago and crossing the river, then ducking into a parking garage at Water Tower Place.

So, I thought, "these self-denying sons of abstinence"[194] occasionally stop into Marshall Field's for a pack of Frango mints. But when I caught up with him, which was not hard thanks to his brilliant orange robe, he was in line at FoodLife, the mall's dining court. Eve was with him, holding a tray with a plate piled high with plain brown

---

[193] Spencer Chapman, *Lhasa* (London: Chatto & Windus, 1940).

[194] C. Markham, Ed. *Narratives of the Mission of George Bogle and the Journey of Thomas Manning to Lhasa* (New Delhi: Manjusri Publishing House, 1971), p. 23.

rice. She stood half a foot taller than he, which wasn't the case the day before. Eve Jablom, timorous librarian, had a pair of stiletto heels on her little feet. I ordered a cranberry sports beverage to keep up my electrolytes.[195]

Eve and the monk ate at a small table, their knees almost touching. When they were done with their food, he produced from his purse a small book, small and charred around the edges.[196] He must have been telling her that it was a book of poems saved from the ravages of the Chinese invasion of Tibet, a place he definitely had never seen, the exile having begun thirty-six years ago. Eve held her hands to her bosom to show she was overcome with gratitude, and, nearly weeping, she pulled out of her bag a large devotional candle of an irregular pyramidal shape.

## Friday 3 March

Nobody can doubt Jung's judgment, "The most beautiful mandalas are, of course, those of the East, especially those belonging to Tibetan Buddhism."[197] The sand mandala is taking form on the lowest floor of the library. A deep-blue God with four faces, each face with three eyes. His twelve hands dance around him. With one outstretched leg he crushes the head of a figure with four

---

[195] The vendors in the food court consider actual money to be too filthy for their antiseptic ambiance. Instead they use plastic debit cards with magnetic strips: invisible pushes and pulls of energy in exchange for solid foods.

[196] A recent issue of the *Times Literary Supplement* (February 3, 1995) profiles a French artist named Denise A. Aubertin, who pours delicate sauces over her favorite books and bakes them in the oven.

[197] *Psyche and Symbol*, pp. 318-19.

arms. Another holds a club on which are fixed a severed head, another in a state of putrefaction, and a gleaming white skull. "The deformed faces signify the denial of all theories," an Italian expert has deduced.[198] The god gnashes his teeth and wrinkles his eyebrows. His eyes and eyebrows flame. He is crowned with five skulls and is adorned with a garland made of fifteen freshly severed heads. His body is blue and naked; his penis, engorged.[199]

Jewels, snakes, lotuses, and feathers of every color encircle the god. Painstakingly, the monks draw in sand an elephant skin, a drum, a hatchet, a knife, a trident, a cranium full of blood, and an apron of tiger skins. A book lies open, its pages burning bloody red.

A crowd of onlookers has gathered. A small child cries lengthily, and a man with a camcorder asks a guard to request that the monks smile, please.

### Saturday 4 March

I can no longer think of a single good reason for carrying out this affront to learning, this travesty of artistic expression, this outrage to the city. Forget it, forget the whole thing.

### Sunday 5 March

I am leaving now.

I am on the bus. Excuse the handwriting. The gym bag containing the bomb is zipped up to my good wrist.

---

[198] Giuseppe Tucci, *The Theory and Practice of the Mandala* (London: Rider, 1961), p. 71.

[199] Tucci states, "The erect penis means that he is consubstantial with the Supreme Beatitude" (p. 73).

I am in the library now, on the seventh floor amidst the humor books, having handed the note to Eve in person with my free hand. The idea to drop it in the return slot along with the videotape wouldn't have worked; I would have grown hungry or sleepy before it was discovered.

"Did you see the mandala," she asked me as I gave it to her.

"Very powerful, very moving."

"You know a lot about art, right? There's a book I want to show you, it's—"

I dashed for the stairs before she could read the note.

"To: The Chicago Public Library

"Attention: Eve Jablom

"Call me Omar. Do as I say and nobody gets hurt. I have on my person a substantial explosive device, and there is only one thing that will keep me from detonating it and destroying the library and all its books: the three area network affiliates and Fox must all simultaneously broadcast the short film, *The Lord's Prayer,* a videotape of which is attached to this note, at nine o' clock tonight. Nothing good is on then, and anyhow the film only takes about six minutes."

An alarm is screaming somewhere, and people are pouring out into the street. They can go. I'm holding all these books hostage.

The Omar thing comes from something Emerson said: "Plato only is entitled to Omar's fanatical compliment to the Koran, when he said, 'Burn the libraries, for their value is in this book.'"[200] I am another Omar, only this one has

---

[200] *Representative Men* (Boston: Phillips, Sampson, & Co., 1850), p. 43.

no Koran and no Plato. I acknowledge blame as a reader for never having found any literature that really satisfied me. I made lists of books and searched them out, somehow hoping to find in one of them a chapter or passage that would bring an end to searching. If you don't find what you're looking for, how do you know when to stop looking?

It feels like a long time has passed, but I'm not certain, since I've been reading. Finally, it makes no difference what book I reach for, because any page I open to contains a sentence that exactly summarizes my feelings, and therefore I must not be feeling anything specific at all. According to Yves Bonnefoy, Arthur Rimbaud "spiritualized his emotional disintegration."[201] Edith Wharton writes, "I was getting to know him too well to express either wonder or gratitude at his keeping his appointment."[202] As I prepare to release my grip on the curling iron, the monks gather outside the library praying for my soul and shivering behind a yellow ribbon: POLICE LINE DO NOT CROSS. Eve watches her friend and admires his piety and his compassion, and yet she is distantly troubled by the unsure recollection of one regular library patron with good manners and an uneasy smile. She would have liked to have gotten to know him better, to talk about favorite books. My ballpoint skips as I write two last lines.

Shema yisrael adonai eloheinu adonai echad!
Baruch shem kavod malchuto leolam va'ed!

[201] *Rimbaud* (New York: Harper Colophon, 1973), p. 37.
[202] *Ethan Frome* (New York: Charles Scribner's Sons), p. 10.

THIS ISSUE IN FOUR SECTIONS

# READER

Friday, August 5, 1994    Volume 23, No. 44    CHICAGO'S FREE WEEKLY

# BUILDING
# BOOM

*In which Chicago architects
identify the buildings they'd most like to blow up.*

**By Cate Plys**

Imagine the rush if you could take a building you really hated and just blow it up.

Technically, you already can. On March 23, the Chicago City Council passed Mayor Daley's proposal to allow the use of explosives for demolition. All you have to do is own the building (a bothersome necessity), fill out the forms, and get about $30 million of insurance—"because we don't want everybody and his brother being able to implode buildings in Chicago," pointed out assistant commissioner John V. Kallianis of the city's Department of Buildings.

But in Chicago, the staggering number

of suitable candidates could paralyze even the most trigger-happy among us. We need guidance. And who better to advise us on which buildings to torch but the very people who design them?

So we asked Chicago architects. If you could pick a building anywhere in Chicago and blow it up, which one would it be?

Most of them were ecstatic.

"Does this include inhabitants?" asked John Macsai, a veteran architect at O'Donnell Wicklund Pigozzi and Peterson (known more simply as OWP&P). "I would blow up some government buildings. Maybe the post office . . ."

"I *love* this idea! I might blow up one of

my own buildings," he enthused.

Some people weren't as comfortable with the proposal.

"I'm not going to answer that because it's an irresponsible question," snapped Jack Hartray of Nagle, Hartray & Associates, Ltd., the firm that designed the new Greyhound bus terminal. Then he softened up a little. "It's so hard to build buildings . . . and there's too much suffering in doing all of this. It's too much work."

"He thinks it's wonderful, but he's reluctant to publicly name a building to blow up," said Thomas Beeby's secretary. Beeby designed the Harold Washington Library. "He suggests you call Stanley Tigerman."

continued on page 14

Mark Swartz is a Chicago writer living in Brooklyn. His fiction, essays, and satire have appeared in *The Chicago Reader, New Art Examiner,* the *Mississippi Review,* the *Brooklyn Rail,* and *Perfect Sound Forever*. This is his first novel.